BUYER BEWARE

Shadow

BUYER BEWARE

FIRST EDITION

A Boner Book by
The Nazca Plains Corporation
Las Vegas, Nevada
2006

ISBN:1-887895-61-2
Published by

The Nazca Plains Corporation ®
4640 Paradise Rd, Suite 141
Las Vegas NV 89109-8000

PUBLISHER'S NOTE
Buyer Beware is a work of fiction created wholly by the author's imagination. All characters are fictional and any resemblance to any persons living or deceased is purely by accident. No portion of this book reflects any real person or events.

Editor Steve Geary
Art Direction Blake Stephens
Cover....

DEDICATION

To all those who took the time to tie me up, and to the sexy skinhead top who crushed my nuts 'til I agreed to try and get my work published -- thanks, sir.

CONTENTS

A Boner Book

BUYER BEWARE

I drove along the street, keeping an eye out for the address my friend had given me. It was a lazy Friday afternoon, so there wasn't too much traffic. Against all the odds, there was apparently a fairly awesome sex shop hidden along this quiet-looking street. I eventually found it and was immediately impressed by its concealment -- merely an unassuming street number on the front of a normal looking building -- none of the usual flashing lights and gaudy signs that usually denoted this type of shop.

Underground off-street parking was also available, obviously for those people who make themselves stand out more before they enter sex shops by frantically looking left and right before entering one. I turned into the parking lot and was surprised at the number of cars already down there; clearly, this place had very good word of mouth.

I entered the front of the store and that was pretty much where the subtle and muted tones ended. Right at the front of the store was a cage with a dude in it. I stopped and watched for a while, not that the guy would know, of course; he was fairly occupied. His head was encased in a tight rubber hood -- no eye or mouth holes, and only two small tubes for the nose. He was breathing heavily through these and causing a faint whistling noise; a heavy collar around his neck with 'D' rings on the sides looked like they were for securing busy hands. This wasn't necessary because he was in a rubber strait jacket.

I admired the shiny material that was obviously rather strong, because this lad had a handsome, muscular build. He was naked below the waist except for his ankles, which were bound together by some ankle restraints and a cb3000, which was doing a good job of containing a monster cock. The cock was a very uncomfortable looking purple color. The cage had a padded bottom and was wide enough to allow him to rock onto his side, but not wide enough to let him roll all the way over. He would be very comfortable if he was lying still; instead, he was frantically bucking his hips and struggling against the restraints of the jacket. It was fun to watch for a while, but the rest of the shop was putting out a siren call that I could no longer resist, so I ventured further back.

The shop was very impressive. There was a path down the middle, with very defined mannequins dressed in an assort-ment of whatever was down the line of shelves they stood in front of. Further down, there were small tables with assorted dildos and plugs on them. If tasteful was a word that could be applied to a sex shop, it would be used to describe this one's layout. I glanced at the mannequins near the front as I strolled down; they were dressed in assorted leather pieces and hoods. These gave way to fetish clothing, army uniforms, police uniforms, etc., and then, nearest to the counter -- black, shiny rubber. I slowed my pace and admired each of these. The rubber was polished to such a sheen they nearly glowed. There were tight vests, chaps, and hoods.

I was running my eye over a torso mannequin dressed in a maroon rubber t-shirt and a rubber choker with a rubber ball gag in its blank face when a cute shop assistant bounced up beside me. I glanced at him; he was wearing a black mesh midriff and cut-off denim shorts. He was my height and looked around my age (twenty-three), had my build (slim with definition in the legs and pecs, and smooth stomach, but no six-pack.) He gave me a lazy grin.

"Hot, isn't it?"

I grinned back. "Yeah, I love rubber. Which reminds me,

how do you apply for that position in the cage? Is there an ad in the paper I should look out for?"

He gave a laugh. "Nah, he's a regular's boy, in for an endurance test. It's been nine hours and he is starting to get a little sick of it, I think. Unfortunately, his top isn't coming to pick him up until tomorrow morning."

I chatted some more with this cute store attendant about general interests. His name turned out to be Trevor. We shared a lot; we were both into rubber and long-term restraint. We were both bottoms. Then he asked me if I was just a browser, playing a bit of pocket pool, or if I had come to buy something.

"Actually, I am after a certain type of rubber gasmask that I have been looking for everywhere." I described it to him -- sleek with the eyes slightly wider apart than most, no tube but a short brass valve.

Trevor listened, nodding, then smiled. "You're in luck, Mike. We just got a shipment of those Russian-style gasmasks in today. A lot of people have been chasing them. We haven't even unpacked them yet. Come check them out."

He led me through the store to the back, through a door marked 'Staff Only' and into the back loading dock area. There were various crates here and there. Trev started digging through a few of them. We kept chatting while he searched. He was finishing soon and had a big play session planned which included a gasmask just like the one I was after.

He gave a grunt of satisfaction and pulled out a mask. My heart gave a leap; it was exactly what I was after. He tossed it to me and I turned it over. He also tossed me another rubber item which turned out to be a 'bit' gag. "They go together well. Those gags are comfy for longer term sessions because they don't stretch the jaw too much, but trying to make any coherent noises with it in is nearly impossible."

I nodded and turned it over in my hand. I told him I would take both and he nodded. "Hang a sec, and I will throw in a bottle of polish for free since you have such awesome taste." He told me to wait while he ducked back into the front of the shop. I handed him my card so he could ring everything up while he was in there.

I'd planned to try and keep him chatting out here for a while longer to see if I couldn't score a play session with him one time. If he was a pure bottom, I would probably be happy to top him, although I really prefer to bottom myself.

I looked around the loading dock area and a flash of light in the corner caught my eye. I noticed it came from a mirror reflecting the outside light coming through the partially-open back door. I strolled over to the mirror and slipped the gag on. The bit sat comfortably in my mouth.

Trev was right, it was impossible to make any noise that was decipherable in it. I glanced down at the hood in my hands. I had waited so long to get one that I couldn't wait another minute to see what it would be like. I pulled it on. It was tight and I had a little trouble getting it to sit comfortably over my ears. I tugged, pulled a little more, and soon had it fitting nicely. I checked out my reflection in the mirror and instantly got hard; the black hood looked awesome against my tight, white t-shirt and baggy blue jeans.

I was just about to pull it off when the back door to the loading dock was opened and a guy rushed in. I was surprised, and spun around. He was about my height, but that's where the similarities ended. This guy was super pumped, and I very much doubted that it had been achieved without the help of some sort of steroids, but he moved with such energy and had such an open, friendly face, that made up for his physical intimidation. He spotted me and didn't seem surprised; in fact, he bounded over to me. I was so shocked at this approach that I was rooted to the spot.

"Ah, Trev, I didn't think you would be ready. I know you were expecting Josh, but he couldn't make it. He will pick you up from the factory when you're all ready. Oh yeah, he says he's sorry if you have been trying to ring him but his mobile is fucked."

He spun me around, grabbed my wrists and it was only then that I snapped out of my immobility. This dude thought I was Trevor!

I tried to struggle and tried to make any kind of sense through my gag. I cursed myself for not taking the three seconds to take it off. The dude stopped what he was doing. "Geez, I forgot how much you like to get 'into' the scene. Fine, I will play along, but I really am in a bit of a hurry, dude."

He pushed me up against the wall and knocked the wind out of me. While I gasped for breath, he pulled my hands together and I felt metal cuffs tightly attached nearly to the point of causing me to cry out in pain. Then, suddenly, I was turned back around, picked up and slung over this dude's shoulder. "There, ya happy? Now, let's get going. Your weekend of fun is waiting."

He was holding me in place with one arm and grasping my legs together with the other. Trying to kick him would probably have been a bad idea because he might have thought 'Trevor' wanted to play harder.

I was momentarily blinded as we entered into the sunlight.

Then my eyes adjusted.

We stopped. He had obviously parked right up against the back of the shop. I heard a door open and I was unceremoniously dumped in the back of a jeep. This caught me slightly off guard and I was momentarily stunned. He grabbed a thick pair of leather ankle restraints and strapped them around my ankles and over my jeans. Then he slammed the back of the jeep shut and jumped into the driver's side. I felt the jeep start off, then lurch slightly as we took off. He wasn't kidding about being in a hurry!

As we whizzed along to who-knows-where, my mind was spinning. This was one hell of a fuck-up! I tried to calm down. There would really be no mistaking me for Trevor once they took my mask off, and no doubt Trevor would wonder where the fuck his ride was when he finished, and if he thought about it really hard, it might work out why I had mysteriously left my credit card and done a runner. No doubt he would call the dude who was supposed to pick him up. But -- this dude had said that 'Josh,' whoever the fuck that was, didn't have a working mobile at the moment, so I would have to wait for them to take the hood off.

I tried to relax as I was tossed around in the back of the jeep. I tried to reach the ankle restraints with my cuffed hands. If I made enough fuss, they might get sore. Unfortunately, I couldn't reach the clips on the restraints with my fingers and soon gave up.

After what seemed like an eternity, I felt the jeep come to a stop and the engine shut off. A few seconds later, the back door was opened and the dude again picked me up and slung me over his shoulder. I had to admit, being manhandled like this was a bit of a turn-on.

He chatted as he walked me to wherever the fuck we

were going. "I am gonna be at the party tonight. Can't wait to see you in your new outfit. I gotta admit, dude, I couldn't do half the shit you can -- like agreeing with Josh to be in that mask from the start of the weekend until the end! Phew, fuck that."

He kept chatting about some other crap, but I was no longer listening. My heart had not only stopped beating but had frozen into a solid block of ice. Trev had agreed to a whole weekend masked and gagged?!?! I noticed that we had entered a building and I could hear the guy calling out to people around him. I couldn't see anything except his back; the mask gave the wearer slight tunnel vision.

I was placed in a chair, and with a nod, a cheeky grin and a wave to me, my kidnapper took off. I tried to get up, but strong hands pulled me back into the chair. I noticed it was sort of an old-style dentist chair but covered in thick black leather. I felt hands uncuff my wrists, but before I could move a single finger, more hands grabbed my wrists and they buckled restraints around them, then attached them to the chair sides with clips.

Soon I was laid back in the chair looking up. There was an older dude standing near a table. All around me, guys were standing around getting stuff ready. The older guy looked over and saw that my hands had been attached to the chair sides and nodded. "OK, you guys, go get the other ones ready. I will start with this one. Bret, uncuff his ankles and get his jeans off, will ya?"

The guys all moved away except for the one that must be Bret, who unbuckled the restraints around my legs. He quickly tugged my jeans down, trapping my legs and preventing me from kicking too much. Then he placed the ankle restraints back on, but this time they were attached to either end of a spreader bar about a foot-and-a-half long and then somehow attached this to the chair.

I had no idea what was going on. My cock was exposed (I don't wear undies) and half-hard. Bret gave it an appreciative glance and then headed off. The guy turned around again from his table. When he saw my cock, he raised an eyebrow and made an annoyed sound. "Damn it, haven't these guys ever heard of a ruler? Six inches, he tells me. If that's six inches, I'll eat my fucking boots."

I was half surprised. My nine-inch endowment often elicited many comments, but few negative ones. He sighed and then pulled the table he had been busy with over to the side of the chair. I tried to tell him there had been a mistake, but he ignored me. He snapped on a pair of latex gloves and picked up what looked like a thick metal cock ring off the table. He whistled to himself as he pulled my cock and balls through it, none too gently, mind you. I winced as he pushed particularly hard on my right nut.

Because I was sitting up, I had a fairly good view. The cock ring was really thick and had a weird sort of bubble at the bottom of it. Next, he picked up a catheter and in a very no-nonsense manner greased it up and inserted it.

It was that kind of pain that makes you go rigid, and stars appear in front of your eyes. When the stars cleared, I was covered in a cold sweat. I watched the urine that had been in my bladder drain into a bag at the end of the tube. When this was done, he took a clip and clipped it onto the tube about four inches from the tip of my cock. He then cut the tube just below the clip.

He then grabbed a weird pan. It was like one of those kidney-shaped hospital dishes, except that it had a semi-circle part cut out of the inner bend and was slightly bowed. The question was answered when he rested it under my cock and balls. The cut-out allowed my cock and balls to sit in the dish. He moved the end of the catheter tube so that it sat on the other side of the pan. I nearly jumped out of my skin when he held it in place with one hand and poured a warm, black liquid over it from a pan with his other hand.

He made an annoyed noise as I half-jumped. "Cut it out, or I will give you a taste of what that shock ring can do!"

My heart froze again. (This was becoming a regular thing.) What the hell did he mean, shock ring? I watched in horrified fascination as he completely covered my cock and balls with the warm goop. My cock had been at half mast when he put the cockring on but had gone soft from the contact of very warm/hot liquid.

Whatever it was cooled quickly and from the way that he was molding it, it seemed to solidify. He shaped and molded it as it dried until I had a nearly perfect sphere where my cock and balls had been, with the tip of the catheter tube poking out and pointed slightly backwards. It was sort of a dull black color.

He removed the pan and grabbed a bottle and a cloth. He poured the contents of the bottle onto the cloth and then polished my sphere till it was a shiny black of.....RUBBER! He gave a satisfied grunt. "There, that wasn't so bad. YO, BRET! THIS ONE IS DONE!"

He moved me to the side, unclipped my hands, refastened them in front of me and unclipped my ankles from the spreader bar, but left the restraints around my ankles. Bret appeared beside me again and the dude tossed him a small black remote. "Here, he seems like a bit of a handful, but he's got the shock ring on, so just give him a zap if he starts playing silly buggers."

Bret grinned and helped me sit up and put my feet on

the floor. I was so stunned as he led me across the room that I didn't really look around. I contemplated trying to run, but I really didn't want to risk getting my cock and balls zapped. We walked over to an area with a whole heap of gym bags on a table and stopped. Bret gave me a grin. "Well, let's see what we have to get you dressed in."

He moved around the bags, reading the attached tags until he found the one that obviously belonged to me. He gave a grunt and dragged me over to the far wall of the room where there were a whole heap of dressing room-style booths. We entered one and he flipped the curtain across. My horror about all of this was starting to fade a little. It's a little hard to stay scared when you're being handled by hot guys, in what would be considered in any other context a jerk-off situation. The theme for Bret and the other guys I had seen around seemed to be "built, not born." They had that solid build -- not the gym-toned and defined look, but solid muscle.

He opened the bag and tipped its contents onto the bench and inside its rubber prison my cock twitched -- painfully, I might add, since it couldn't grow. A pair of black twenty-hole docs and a large pile of rubber had been in the bag. Bret made a noise of approval in the back of his throat. He then turned, unclipped my wrists and took the restraints off.

I reached up quickly for the mask, but he was quicker. His hands flew to his belt where the remote was and my hands flew down to the rubber sphere encasing my cock as spasms of pain shot through my cock and balls. I was literally kneeling on the floor in agony before he stopped. "Geez, Greame was right. You're a right little handful, aren't you? Let's not try that again, huh?"

I nodded, and I meant it. Any thoughts of trying to get the mask off had fled. I would play along with this and not play up again because that shock had fucking hurt, and I got the impression that it had only been a warning one. I got up a little jelly-legged and Bret pointed a finger to the pile of clothes. He leaned against the wall as I dressed, casually holding the remote for the shock ring in his hand in case I made another attempt at freedom.

I sorted through the clothing and worked out what order I would have to put the stuff on. I grabbed a pair of rubber gloves that came up to my arms and pulled them on. Everything had been dusted with talcum and had that dull grey look of rubber covered in talcum, but I knew once it was polished up I would shine like greased darkness. Once the gloves were on, I pulled on a pair of rubber shorts. It had a reasonably-sized plug built in, nothing I couldn't handle. I located a bottle of lube and lubed the plug up and then squeezed some on my ass. I sat down on the seat, forcing the plug in slowly. This is the best way I have found to insert plugs. Soon, the widest part popped past my sphincter and I stood up and pulled the shorts all the way up, enjoying that warm, full feeling that comes from a butt plug.

The shorts had the crotch missing and I manipulated my sphere through the opening. Next was a cat suit. The opening was in the back and it was a tight fit. Bret helped me slide into the inside of the suit and tugged and pulled the rubber around me. Again there was no crotch in this suit and I manipulated the sphere through. The end of the sleeves were open, but because of the sleeves I would not be able to take the gloves off without first taking off the cat suit.

Bret zipped me up at the back and I felt the rubber suit grip me slightly tighter. He grabbed a small padlock that was in the pile and I heard a click. I knew I was now locked in this suit. The neck of the suit was fairly high, and since the mask came to about halfway down my neck, the two overlapped slightly. I grabbed a collar that was on top of the pile and handed it to Bret.

I didn't want him thinking I was making another bid for freedom when putting the collar on. He fastened it around my neck tightly at the point where the suit and mask overlapped. I was now basically trapped in this outfit.

He had me sit down and put on my boots. There was a pair of long white socks, even though the suit had built-in feet. I laced the boots up and then stood up. I held out my hands so that the last item, a pair of rubber fist mitts, could be fastened on. They had locks on the buckles, and once they were done up, Bret locked them up. I could now not get out of any of my clothing. My hands were useless; my fate was well and truly sealed.

I followed Bret out of the dressing room. This time I had a look around. We were in a large warehouse. The floor area was full of people moving around doing stuff, but everything was sorta temporary -- trestle tables and stuff that suggested they could be moved easily, and over in one corner I saw a band setting up. A bar was being assembled in the other corner. There was obviously going to be a large party here.

Bret led me over to a area near the large entrance. Against the wall, there was a whole heap of black boxes. I realized some had heads poking out of them. One had a gasmask on, another was an inflatable one. The last was a weird sort of dog head-shaped hood; on the front of the boxes were printed names -- 'Boi Ted,' 'Fido,' and, second from the end, 'Slut Trevor.' I realized that was mine.

Bret opened the box. It split into two halves. There was a bench that could be adjusted for height, and manacles on chains to keep the boys' hands from wandering while locked up. Bret adjusted the bench height. Then I sat down, and he fastened my useless hands into the manacles. There was a semi-circle cut out of the front of the bench in the middle and a bucket underneath. Bret positioned my rubber sphere so that it sat in the curve and then removed the clip from the end of the catheter. He stepped back and swung the two halves together. The top sat snugly against my collar, meaning I couldn't turn my head much.

Bret then produced a very serious looking padlock from his pocket and locked it on the front of the box. "There ya go. Only your master has the key to the lock, so no one can steal ya away but him." He gave me a grin and placed the shock control next to my head. "Of course, anyone could wander up and test that out! So you better stay quiet and not draw attention to yourself!" He laughed and wandered off to the band area. I thought of the irony of being so safe from any strangers kidnapping me while I sat in the box. I waited -- but for what?

I sighed and tried to wiggle a little. Whoever had built the box had neglected to pad the bench; then again, I suppose it probably hadn't been unintentional at all. I have no idea how long I was there. The slight horniness I had experienced from being manhandled was now gone. I was sweating in the rubbers like mad. I wanted to get the mask off and I definitely wished to find who had designed this damned bench seat and have a quiet word with him, preferably with a bat.

While I fantasized about slamming a bat against the dude's ass while he was plugged to let him know precisely how uncomfortable this was, I watched what was going on around me. The boxes were all full now, so I was guessing we had to start soon. The majority of people wore standard, full-head hoods, either rubber or leather, some with blindfolds, some without. Everyone was gagged -- either that or just staying quiet.

The band was fully set up now and running through a few songs. One small grace was that they weren't playing 60's or 70's crap; that would have been true torture, unable to escape that while locked in a box. When the slave for the box marked Fido was placed in his box, he had a dog hood on; also, a small tail stuck out the back of his suit. I wondered if his bench had been designed to accommodate that.

The slave two boxes to my left had been put in wearing only a leather g-string and chaps and only had black duct tape over his mouth. However, he wasn't taking this lightly. He was shaking his head and working his jaw furiously trying to get he tape off. This was rather stupid, because each of us had a remote next to our heads. Obviously, we all had the shock rings around our cock and balls. So all he was managing to do was to encourage guys to make use of his, and this seemed to only make him more determined to get out.

I sighed and hoped this all started soon. I went back to my daydream while the dude a few boxes down let out another muffled scream as someone grabbed his remote and shocked him again.

If I had to guess, I would say about half an hour passed before tops began to arrive. Some walked straight past us; others glanced at us and one particularly nasty individual picked up each of our remotes as he walked past and shocked us. After again having a taste of the current that damn ring puts through my genitals, I was more determined than ever to just behave and be good.

Soon the room was full of hot leather tops. There were a few skinhead tops wandering around -- and one unique individual who brought to mind Nurse Betty meets Santa. I put up a little prayer that that wasn't Josh, my apparent top for the evening. Pretty soon there was a full party going. I was a little worried about the number of tops heading to the bar, since drunk tops and electric shock rings do not really make for a happy combo.

Soon enough, a hot leather top bounded onstage and grabbed the microphone as the band finished a song. "All right, all you kinky fuckers, let's get this party started. As you will all have noticed when you arrived, some tops have kindly donated their lads to provide us with some amusement. If everyone will go collect their property and have them line up at the front of the stage here, we can begin the fun."

I watched as a group of tops detached themselves from the crowd and headed toward us. A guy stopped in front of me and started to unlock the padlock. This must have been Josh. He was fairly hot, probably in his early thirties and not a bad bod, from the look of things. He had a short haircut and managed to carry himself in his leather well. He opened the front of the box, squatted down and put a clip around the end of the catheter tube. Undoing my hands from the manacles, he clicked his fingers and made an up motion. I quickly sprang to my feet, not even bothering to try to take the mask off -- no point risking another shock. I followed behind him.

From the sounds of things, the unwilling slave had to be shocked a few times before he behaved himself and followed his top out to the front of the stage. Josh arrived, turned and stood facing the crowd. I quickly knelt in front of him, facing the crowd, and heard him make a noise of approval. When the last slave and master had arranged themselves at the end, I heard the top MC yell out, "Let the gaaaaaaaaames begin!!" Oh, joy.

The games were both amusing and exhausting. There were three dog slaves in the group. They all had their ankles strapped to their calves to make them stay on all fours and then they were led over to an area where a small obstacle course was set up, similar to the ones you see in real dog shows. The poor guys were run through the course with the tops running along beside them, zapping them to encourage them along.

The next game was like Spin the Bottle, except the remotes were all placed in a circle and we all had to stand on the stage. They were all mixed up, so we had no idea which one was actually ours. I vaguely recalled that there was a number on the bottom of each remote, but we couldn't see it from up on the stage. A top would walk into the center of the circle every now and again and he was allowed to spin a bottle. Whichever remote the bottle neck ended up pointing at, he picked up, and then we all waited nervously to see which one of us was unlucky enough to have been chosen.

It was generally fairly easy to tell whose remote had been chosen, and the rest of us got to relax slightly and watch the poor victim squirm on the ground. Individual tops also played with their bottoms. One top kept feeding his boy beer after beer and kept his catheter clamped, then unclipped it. He caught all the drained piss in a glass and promptly fed it back to the boy. One top came up, collected his lad and dragged him into the toilets. I later learned he had been tied down in the urinal, the remote placed on a shelf nearby so that tops could watch him squirm as his balls were shocked while they pissed on him.

I noticed as the games progressed that the dude in just chaps with duct tape over his mouth was becoming more and more agitated. I also noticed that his top was a really young guy. He was also fucking hot -- he couldn't have been much older than twenty and was dressed in leather jeans, black biker boots and a leather vest. He had brown hair, and later on in the night, when I happened to pass him by, bright green eyes flashed out from under his eyelashes. His vest moved aside every now and again to reveal that he had a tattoo above his right pec that said 'Pray'. From the way he laughed at his lad being tortured, it was probably a warning. (If only more tops came with warning labels, or someone had thought to stick a sign over mirrors saying, Remember To Take Off Your Gag Before Placing Gasmask On To Avoid Being Mistaken For Someone Else!)

As I stood, pondering this deep and meaningful revelation,

I felt someone grab me, and I was dragged over near the bar where I saw most of the other bottoms were already standing. All the dogs appeared to have been chained up over in another area. Something was being done to them, but I couldn't see what. I very much doubted that they were being pampered somehow.

The difficult slave had chains added to his wrists and ankles and was lying on the bar. Guys were doing jello shots off him and zapping him when he tried to struggle away. I saw one guy dump a shot over the dude's left nipple, cover the whole area with his mouth, and started to suck and bite, long after the shot had no doubt started its journey to assault his liver and motor functions. I winced in sympathy, but a treacherous thought of 'better him than me' flashed through my mind.

My attention was quickly brought back to the present by Josh shouting in my ear. It was a little hard to understand him with the gasmask on and the music and crowd in the background. I got the basic gist of things, though; I was to carry a tray of drinks around. The tray had a short chain ending in a manacle on it which was attached to my wrist, just below the buckles and locks of the fist mitts. I managed to get a good grip on the tray with my two mitted hands. I noticed a lot of the other slaves had been put in fist mitts, or gloves, that made holding the trays very difficult.

With a yell of "drop the tray, and you will wish you hadn't been born" in my ear, Josh set off toward the dog area. The bar guys had us line up and started to pile drinks onto our trays.

I can't say I was thrilled at the idea of passing out free booze to a crowd that had the potential to send a considerable amount of voltage through my groin. Drunk people have a very odd sense of humor. Plus, the trays were made of heavy metal and already fairly heavy before the drinks were put on them. I did send up a prayer of thanks when I saw the look in the eyes of a slave wearing a piss gag. He was looking down at his tray of drink and probably thinking that, one way or another, he would end up drinking most of this, if not from the bottle, then through a 'straw'.

Moving through the crowd with the heavy trays of drinks was a nightmare. Of course, no one moved aside for us; why would they? I was having enough trouble holding my tray as it was, because my hands were sweating badly under all the rubber, along with the rest of my body. I could feel sweat pooling in the feet of my catsuit. Being constantly bumped, or someone unexpectedly taking a bottle off the tray, or dumping an empty bottle back on, meant that I had to devote my full attention to moving carefully and concentrating on holding the tray. If you think this was an easy task, remember that at any point we could receive a very painful shock to our nuts, though the few jolts I *did* receive were a lot less severe than the previous ones. Obviously, they were giving us a little bit of slack. Also, remember that most of us had appendages that ended in the equivalent of flippers. I thought back to childhood, watching the penguin waiters in Mary Poppins, carrying trays around; the little fuckers made it look easy. I was also having trouble seeing because sweat kept getting in my eyes, stinging like all hell and making my vision blurry.

I did get to see perfectly what happened to a lad who dropped his tray. I'm not sure how it happened, but he was immediately dragged up to the stage, where a nasty set-up had been erected without me noticing. I had been too busy concentrating on my tray, and was now grateful for it.

The boy's legs were tied to the top of a box, about a foot-and-a-half high. Then, a metal plate with a wire that ran to the base of the box was taped to his chest, then another box placed under his chest. This one was a tad shorter than the other box. His hands were then cuffed to a chin-up bar suspended from an A-frame. Basically, he was lying with his stomach resting on one box and his feet on the other and his hands raised slightly. It didn't look all that bad, but for some reason he seemed desperate to keep himself from lying on the box, using the chin-up bar to keep his chest raised above the box. That position looked agonizing. It wasn't until the MC announced that the plate attached to his chest completed a circuit whenever it touched the box under his chest, thus zapping his balls, that his determination to stay off it began to make sense, and made me more determined than ever not to drop my tray, since whoever next dropped their tray would replace him. If no one did for twenty minutes, he would be let out.

I developed a route. I headed straight from the bar to the other side of the room, then back again, turning back earlier if my tray was emptied or filled with empty bottles. I didn't stop, since stationary lads with empty trays made good targets for tops looking to zap someone's nuts.

A well-known mythological figure was condemned to an eternity of pushing a rock up a hill only for it to roll to the bottom again, so he had to push it back up; frankly, he got off easy, in my opinion. He should have tried making his way through a crowd of people jostling him while trying to hold a heavy tray, covered head to toe in rubber, sweat building up under it all, a butt plug up his ass making itself well-known with every step, blurred vision and occasional surprised shocks to his cock and balls.

I was dedicating all my attention to getting from the bar and back again without dropping anything, but I did notice a few things. The first was the top from earlier in the night; he seemed to have his own little personal circle. He was smiling and chatting to others but no one seemed to want to get too close to him. If he was aware of this, it didn't show because he was flashing his white-toothed grin all around.

I went to make use of this absence of people around him

one time and very nearly paid dearly for it; as I passed beside him, he turned his head, which was when I caught a glimpse of his green eyes. At the same time, I felt someone kick me in the ankle of the foot I had just lifted to take a step, causing it to hook around my other ankle and me to very nearly lose my balance and fall flat on my face. I managed to get my foot unhooked and quickly bent my knee, landing heavily on the other. I knew there would be a bruise there later.

Thankfully, my tray, mercifully, was still firmly in my hands. A few bottles seemed to have it out for me as they wobbled ominously, but the others obviously talked them into playing nice, and not having me tortured, as they settled back into position. A few people had noticed this; one or two laughed in a nervous manner, the rest seemed to be more interested in what he would do next. I, too, was under the impression that I would receive a boot in the butt to finish off the forward momentum I had so luckily halted.

Instead, a hand hooked under my armpit and he pulled me back to my feet. I glanced at his face; it was devastatingly handsome. I felt my knees go weak again. There was a somewhat calculating look in his eyes that made me feel like I was about to have a price tag stuck on me. Hopefully it wouldn't say 50% off. He then flashed me a grin and gave me a pat on the butt to send me on my way. I made a note NOT to head anywhere near him again for the rest of the night, even if he didn't try to trip me; another glance from those eyes might be enough to make my legs go out from under me.

The other thing I noticed from my wanderings was the dog pen. All the dog slaves had been put in a small, fenced area. There seemed to be carpeting on the floor, which no doubt would have been a blessing for them, even though they all wore knee pads. They seemed to be happily scampering around the area. There were a few chew toys and some balls in the area. The slaves were basically acting like real dogs would if let off their leashes in an area full of toys.

I envied them for a few seconds until I noticed something -- if any of them stopped for more then a few seconds, there were a few guys around the edge of the pen sitting on chairs happily chatting and drinking. If they saw a stationary mutt, they lifted the remote and zapped the unfortunate pooch, and unlike us, I doubted that their shock rings had been put to a lower setting. Basically, they had to keep moving and playing and romping around. They could never stop acting like they had the energy of real dogs.

Now, crawling around on your hands and knees with your ankles strapped to your calves is not an easy task, and being forced to keep this apparent happy scamper going would be as exhausting as us having to carry these damned trays around. It also seemed that if a dog played with one toy too long or didn't make contact with a ball for more than a few minutes, they also received a shock. The balls themselves seemed to be bouncy rubber and rolled away at the lightest of touches. I began to wonder if maybe I had ended up with the easy end of the deal.

Just as it seemed like my arms would turn to jelly and I would not be able to keep my tray up, thereby losing all the drinks on it and thus being forced to use my already-spent arms to keep my already-aching nuts from being zapped, the party ended. I gratefully sank to the floor, leaning my back against the bar where I had just arrived to receive another load of drinks.

I had no idea how much time had passed. To me, it seemed like I had been forcing my unsteady legs to carry me through the crowd. I couldn't see properly carrying what felt like an armful of lead in front of me for a week, although, chances were, it was probably a lot less than that. I was hot and more than a little sweaty and dying of thirst.

Josh came up to me and squatted down next to me. If he had zapped my balls, I swear I would have kicked him right in the head. I was sick of playing nice; I wanted out. Instead, he patted my head. "Hey, buddy, I'm so proud of you, Trev. You did an awesome job. Hope you're not pissed at me for making you come to the party. I know I promised I wouldn't, but they were short a lad and asked me if I could bring you. Anyway, you will need a drink, so let's get that mask off you."

He reached into his jeans and pulled out a key. He used it unbuckle the fist mitts off me and handed me the key for the collar. While he stood up and turned to the bartender to ask for a drink, I was nearly pissing myself with excitement and fumbling with the lock on the back of the collar, afraid he would turn around and change his mind. After what seemed like forever, I got the collar off and nearly ripped the mask off my head. I didn't care if I destroyed it; I just wanted it off. Thankfully, it was thick rubber and bore my frenzied actions easily.

I sighed with relief as cool air hit me in the face. I rubbed the sweat out of my eyes and reached back. Again, not caring if I destroyed the damned thing, I ripped open the buckle of the gag, pulled it off and took a deep breath of air through my mouth. I rubbed my hair back; it was probably wet with sweat, but I couldn't tell with the gloves on. I stood up, tapped Josh on the shoulder, and prayed he didn't have any pre-existing heart conditions.

Josh turned and looked at me as if waiting to see why someone had tapped him on the shoulder. I held up the mask and grinned. He glanced back at the floor, then back up, with eyes almost perfectly round in amazement as the penny dropped. The look on his face almost made the whole night bearable -- almost.

After a quick explanation, and me promising I wasn't

going to head to the police, and that I hadn't done anything to Trevor, he relaxed. I managed a grin and he suddenly realized that I had gone through all this all night and burst out laughing; at that point, I wished I had a remote for a shock ring around his nuts.

We walked out to his car with him still laughing and apologizing. I would have liked to have completely gotten out of the gear, but Josh told me I would have to get changed at home because he had not brought the key for the lock holding me in the catsuit. After all, he had not intended to take it off Trevor until they got home.

I was carrying the mask in my hand and it slipped out from between my weary fingers. I groaned as I bent down to pick it up and felt the plug move inside me -- couldn't wait for that to come out, either!

As I glanced up, I saw that the hot top with the unwilling boy was standing near the entrance, talking to a muscular figure I identified as Bret. They seemed to be looking in my direction. In other circumstances, I might have been happy to be the attention of two hot guys; however, all I was concerned about at the moment was getting my hands on the key to get me out of this suit, so I straightened up and headed toward Josh standing beside his jeep.

As I climbed in, I looked around and thought this was probably the only time in my life that wandering through a car park, in a skintight rubber catsuit and 20 hole boots, with a gasmask and gag dangling from my hand, would not draw a lot of attention.

On the trip to his house, Josh got me to tell him over and over about how I had been snagged from the back of the shop by a mysterious assailant, whose name, I learned, was Damien. He laughed as I told him about my few attempts to get the mask off. "Well, Mike, Trevor will probably thank you. He made me swear I wouldn't make him participate in that party." Yep, that's me, folks, -- do'er of good deeds.

I noticed that the clock on the dash said it was 1:30 in the morning. It had been about two when I went into the shops; I had been like this for nearly twelve hours.

We pulled up to the front of Josh's house, and sitting on the doorstep was none other than Trevor. His eyes went huge when he saw me, and a quick explanation cleared everything up. There was a quick phone call to Damien and a lot of laughing, in which I did not participate.

Josh handed me the key to the suit and the bag which had all my clothes in it. It seemed like an eternity since I had been stripped down and encased in rubber. He also handed me a small bottle and told me I had to soak my rubber-encased cock in a bucket of warm water which I was to tip this into; it would make it brittle enough to crack off in about half a hour.

Trevor came into the bathroom while I was squatting over the bucket of water with my rubber sphere soaking in it. I was naked and enjoying the feel of it. We chatted for a while and he got me to tell him all about the night. None of this was his fault, so I really didn't mind that he laughed; plus, he was hot. He had taken off his shirt, saying that he felt hot because the hot water had steamed up the room -- a likely excuse. While we chatted, he casually moved closer, and when my watch beeped to tell me that it had been half an hour, I stood up and he offered to help me get the sphere off.

The rubber had indeed gone very brittle. A sharp tap with a bottle was enough to crack it. As he helped me get the rest of the rubber off, his hands seemed to be on my cock more than the rubber, and since it was finally free and being stimulated, my cock rose to attention and Trevor nodded in appreciation. "Fuck, you will need to get soft to get that cock ring off."

I smiled back at him. "Yeah, I usually start to go soft after I cum." He grinned at me. I leaned back against a counter and groaned with pleasure as I felt his warm mouth close over my poor cock, which had suffered a terrible evening.

I would like to say it was a long, erotic scene with our bodies withering against each other. Unfortunately, I was horny as all fuck, and he was a good cocksucker. No more than five minutes later, he was wiping his mouth and I was starting to droop.

After I slipped the cursed ring off and considered that I would very much like a chance to cram it up the ass of the old fart who had slipped it around me in the first place, Trev suddenly pulled me towards the shower.

Now I can describe a scene of two bodies rubbing against each other while steam whirled, making exotic patterns in the air also heavy with lust. Trev soaped me down and moved behind me, rubbed me gently on the back and pressed himself against me to reach around to soap up my chest. I leaned my head back and found his mouth waiting for mine; I turned to face him and he drew me into a hot embrace. We stood like that for a while with the warm water showering over us while we kissed, and his tongue battled against mine for territory in the other's mouth. His stiff manhood pressed up against my nude crotch. I slipped a soapy hand between us and rubbed his cock while I felt my own spent member begin to rise up again, gradually running up the inside of his leg. He eventually shuddered, gasped, pulled me tight against him and came, the hot sticky liquid trapped in the gap between our bodies.

We laughed, rinsed off, kissed and then hopped out of the shower. When we had finished toweling ourselves dry, neither of us made any move to dress. I was ready for bed. It was after two in the morning, I was exhausted, and had no desire to sleep in jeans. Josh had already told me I was staying the night, and Trev could drop me off tomorrow when he went to let in the top who was coming to pick up his rubber lad from the cage in the front of the store.

It seemed like a year since I had stood watching that helpless lad, clueless that I, myself, was about to be made just as helpless, if not more so. We slipped into bed together, and Trev snuggled up behind me as I lay on my side. My eyes grew heavy and I simply drifted off to sleep. It had been one VERY long day.

I was up by about 8 in the morning, which is surprising, since not only do I like to sleep in on Saturdays, but considering what I had been through the night before, I figured I was going to need at least three days' sleep to get over it. However, with a little less than six hours' sleep under my belt, I felt fine.

I got up and pulled on my jeans and shirt that were near the bed. I pulled my boots on and headed into the kitchen. Josh was sitting at the table while Trev was cooking eggs and bacon. He was in the catsuit I had been trapped in last night, with an apron over the top to protect it from grease splatter. I sat down as they both said good morning.

Josh was obviously telling Trev about some of the people they must both know who were at the party. "So, John was there with Andrew. Those poor guys were as exhausted as everyone else after running round in the pen all night. Joe was meant to have Pete with him, but he was sick, which is why they asked me to bring you. Lucky Mike rocked up and did your job for you. Oh, and of course, Tommy turned up with some straight lad."

The way he said this last part caught my attention, which had previously been attuned to focusing on how cute Trev's butt looking in the cat suit. Trev also turned around. "Oh what, don't tell me -- he's been pushing everyone around again?"

Josh nodded. The suggestion on his face suggested that he had swallowed something unpleasant. My curiosity had been piqued, so I voiced the obvious question. "Who is Tommy?"

Josh glanced over at me, realizing I probably had no idea who they were talking about. "He's the guy who rocked up with the slave in the chaps and tape over his mouth -- probably not even a slave, probably not even gay. Tommy has an odd sense of humor sometimes."

My mind immediately conjured up a picture of green eyes above an almost angelic smile, and my cock stirred slightly in my jeans. I definitely wanted to know more about him, but I sensed that expressing interest would not be the way to go about it, so I pretended for casual curiosity. "So, why do you guys put up with him? He looked fairly young to me."

At this, Josh gave a snort. "Yeah, he is young -- only about twenty. Thing is, though, he's connected."

The way he said it gave me the impression he meant he could do more than make sure you got a discount at certain stores. My suspicions were confirmed as Josh continued talking. "He had two older brothers who were running the operations. Both of them got taken out in a police shoot last year during a drug bust. Everyone thought Tommy wouldn't be able to cut it -- turns out everyone was wrong. He may look all cute and innocent with that big smile of his, but he is one dangerous customer. He is ruthless and determined. If he is crossed, he doesn't just take out the person who crossed him; he also takes out the guy's friends and family. Also, he has a thing for young, cute gays. Every now and again a guy will go missing and rock up a few days later, fairly worse for wear -- nothing serious, no broken bones or anything. We'd all know it was him, but the guys are too scared to speak up and the police can't touch him."

Suddenly I was feeling that maybe those piercing dark eyes were not as hot as previously thought. It's all well to have the smile and face of an angel, but when demons dance in the depths of your eyes, it's a whole different kettle of fish. For some reason, though, whenever I thought back to him looking at me, my cock stirred in my jeans. As always, a guy's cock doesn't care how smart it is to be attracted to someone -- only how hot the person is.

I tried to put it out of my mind as I ate breakfast, and soon I had forgotten about it because I was so damned hungry.

"We don't open 'til 6pm on weekends," Trev said, "but that dude's top is gonna be here soon. Actually, I think I see him up there now. Keep in touch, okay?"

I said I would, and hopped out and headed down the ramp to the car park while Trev hurried up to the entrance of the store to let in the top to retrieve his lad. He had been told by Josh to get it done quickly and get back because he had a whole day of missed rubber encasement to make up for.

I strolled down the ramp to the car park, which was empty except for my car. All the lights in the car park were off. I assumed it was because the store was closed. Thankfully, I had parked not too far from the ramp, where enough light came down to allow me to find the keyhole in the door. I opened the door and hopped in, throwing a small bag containing my gasmask and gag onto the passenger seat.

As I did so, I noticed an envelope on the seat. I was sure I hadn't left one there. Then I realized I had left my keys and wallet yesterday when being kidnapped -- Damien had probably come around earlier in the morning to drop them off, and maybe Trev had written a note telling me where to contact him when I came back for my car. I opened the letter, but instead of some angry or curious note from Trev telling me to contact him for my wallet back, there were just four words in big thick lettering -- DEEP BREATHS NOW, SLUT.

I was just thinking that sounded a little cryptic for a note telling me where to find my wallet when an arm came from around the headrest and clamped a cloth over my mouth and nose. I gasped in shock and immediately smelled something sweet. That's about all I remember; after that, it was just darkness.

I groaned and tried to open my eyes. Unfortunately, I seemed as coordinated as a six-legged spider on an acid trip. While I still tried to convince my eyes to open, I managed to push myself up onto my elbows and tried to sit up. Unfortunately, I whacked my head against a hard surface and went straight back down again. I lay there for a few seconds until my mind reached a decision regarding precisely which was up. I slowly sat up again, having finally resisted the urge to cling to the floor for fear of falling off it. This time, when I felt my head hit the surface above me, I slowly rolled over and managed to prop myself up on all fours. My stomach briefly considered throwing up, but thankfully decided to hold out on this decision for a little while longer.

I managed to get my eyes open and was thankful that wherever I was, it was reasonably dim; I wasn't sure how well my eyes would take bright light at this point. Slowly, the blurs and blobs managed to join and stretch into actual images. This is not to say that things got better from that point on, mind you, merely that I could see.

The first thing that I noticed was that I was in a cage -- not a prison, but a cage. The bottom was padded leather, and it was high enough to let me kneel if I bent my head right over -- not a position I wanted to try, considering my stomach seemed to be a on the brink of leaving my body. A lap full of vomit would not make this situation any better. I chose instead to lay back down, but on my stomach, and examine the next thing which had caught my attention. It was a man.

He was standing not so far away from me. He, like me, did not seem to be having the best of days. He was spread in an 'X' shape, his arms attached to chains that seemed to lead up to the roof. His ankles had heavy metal manacles around them which were secured to iron rings in the floor. His back was a criss-cross of red marks; he had obviously been whipped.

I was viewing him from behind. His head was bowed and his whole body was limp. I could see his chest expand and contract, suggesting that he was breathing. Nothing about this situation was really good for confidence, but it would have been made far worse by the presence of a corpse.

The general theme of the room's furniture suggested a dungeon. My cage was locked with a heavy padlock. I was buck naked, and, in any event, even if I had been wearing a hairpin I very much doubted I could have suddenly learned how to pick a lock in time. Because the room's only other occupant wasn't in a talkative mood and I was in no immediate danger and still not feeling great, I rolled back onto my side and managed to fall back asleep.

As unlikely as that may seem, remember my previous day's activities (I was going on the assumption that it was still the same day) and the fact that I was still feeling the effects of whatever they knocked me out with.

I snapped awake again, and this time, my eyes opened and regarded the roof of my cage. There was no grogginess now, and with a clear mind, panic decided to take the place of drug-addled confusion. I had a newfound understanding for junkies, though I would bet coming down for them didn't involve this sort of thing. My heart was slamming against my ribcage and I again rolled onto my side, this time thinking all sorts of irrational things, like maybe I could chew my way through the bars.

As I rolled over, I realized what had caused me to wake up -- the sound of moaning and rattling on chains. This, however, was not due to any poltergeist activity.

I saw, also, that there was yet another person in the room -- bare, broad shoulders, some sort of tattoo on his back, legs and ass encased in tight leather jeans and heavy boots on his feet. He was standing with his back to me as well. He was tenderly stroking the guy's back and talking softly into his ear. The actions seemed almost tender, until you realized the guy was fighting the restraints, shaking his head and moaning loudly.

This made the whole scene sinister. A sense of terrible power seemed to be contained in the leather guy's whole body. I was mesmerized by his hand gently stroking the tortured back of the chained dude, and I had very little doubt as to who was responsible for him being there.

He stepped back from the figure and waved off to the side. I saw two dark figures suddenly appear and head toward my fellow captive; his moans increased at this point.

I really wasn't paying attention, though. The figure had turned toward me -- a bright, wide and friendly smile, and two piercing green eyes.

I was frozen where I was. Even if I had been free, I doubt I could have run. I was like a deer trapped in the glare of oncoming headlights. Like that noble creature, a certainty suddenly took hold of me; I was staring into my doom. The figure strolled forward and squatted down in front of my bars. Suddenly I was very happy to be in my cage, mainly because it served to keep certain things out.

He regarded me for a few seconds with an amused expression. No doubt my face wore an expression of extreme shock. He flashed that devastatingly friendly smile at me and held his hand through the bars. "Hi, I don't think we've been introduced properly, Mike. I am Tommy." I reached forward and shook his hand. He withdrew it and regarded me for a while longer. I didn't trust myself to speak, so I chose silence instead. His smile again appeared like a thousand-watt bulb suddenly flaring into existence. "Well, this is a little awkward. We should get to know each other a little better over dinner." With that, he stood up and walked out swiftly.

At this point, I noticed two things -- one was that the chained guy had gone. The other was that a guy that looked like, somewhere in his past, one of the providers for his maternal genes had gotten it on with a bull, was approaching my cage.

At any other stage in my life, I would probably have been thrilled to be walking beside a muscled hunk like the one that was leading me down the hall. At any other stage, however, I would probably not have had heavy metal chains connecting two manacles around my wrists and another set connecting a pair around my ankles. I could walk easily; there was plenty of chain.

But fleeing was a stupid idea; the hulk beside me could probably snap me with his little finger. Another reason was that around my neck was a metal collar. There was a chain connected to it which was clutched in the hand of my escort. I had been given a pair of leather shorts to wear; they had lacing up the sides of the legs and were very short.

We seemed to be in a large house. It had been a little surprising to step off the cold stone floor of the dim dungeon into a brightly lit hallway with deep carpeting. We walked up to a door and then through it into a dining room. There was a large oak table in the center which could easily seat about twenty people.

Seated near the middle was Tommy. I was led around to the other side directly opposite him and the chair was pulled out for me. I sank into it and felt him doing something with the chain to my collar. I heard a click and then the muscled thug left the room. I didn't need to put my hand behind me to know that my chain had been locked to the chair.

Tommy was grinning at me again and I felt my cock twitch inside its leather confinement. I also felt like a fish looking out of its bowl at a cat. He leaned back in his chair, one arm lazily slung over the back of it. He had put on a loose, white shirt with a really low 'V' collar. He looked fucking hot, there was no denying it; even mice can probably agree that snakes have style.

"You were tricky to track down, Mike. I knew something was up when I saw the look in your eyes last night at the party. I asked around and everyone thought you were Jon's lad Trevor, but I had seen Trevor in action. He's more of a poser. Something about you suggested much more."

At this stage, a maid appeared with plates of food. I was instantly mortified about a chick seeing me like this. She didn't even bat an eyelid as she placed a plate of food in front of me. There was a knife, fork, and spoon. The idea of trying to stab Tommy didn't even cross my mind; it would have been a better idea to dig my grave with my spoon. Tommy motioned for me to eat and I did so. I was hungry and the food smelled good.

He continued to talk while I chewed through my plate of food. "I saw the little scene at the bar where your mask came off. I managed to track down Bret, who had handled you, who told me that Damien had dropped you off. I had a little chat with Damien. He is very scared of me, and with good reason. Anyway, he proved very helpful, showed me where you had parked and everything, so I decided to invite you over for a play. After dinner, we can move back to the dungeon and continue there."

Suddenly, my appetite was not so great. "You're in luck," he continued. "I have spent most of the day working over the individual who I took to the party last night. His behavior was really inexcusable, made me look bad, and I don't like that." A shiver ran up my spine. "He's now on his way to spend the night in a sling at an S&M club. No doubt he will be fucked and fisted all night long. Since he is straight, this may be rather uncomfortable. Thankfully, he will be gagged and locked in the sling, so he won't be able to cause too much fuss. I am sure I will be able to find the energy to provide you with a fun scene, though, Mike."

Another flash of that smile and again my cock twitched; lust is a terrible thing. He bent forward and began to eat. I continued to do so as well, sure I would need the energy. I tried not to dwell too much on what lay ahead.

After dinner, Tommy stood up, walked around and stood behind me. I had been frozen stiff in terror and trembling with lust. He reached down and tenderly ran a hand over my chest, rubbing his thumbs over my nipples. I gasped, and my cock immediately bulged out against the leather of the shorts. I closed my eyes and leaned back as he continued to run his hands over my body. I wanted him so badly.

His soft caress continued. I shivered, anticipating that at any second he would suddenly pinch my nipples hard or slap me or something. Instead, I suddenly felt a pair of soft lips press against mine. My eyes flew open in surprise. His handsome face was right there in front of mine. Those killer eyes were closed, thankfully, or else it's likely I would have melted. As it was, my whole body relaxed; I allowed my mouth to open slightly and I pushed my tongue forward to meet his. Gently, he flicked his tongue against my lips and nibbled playfully on my lip -- unusually tender for the sort of person he was.

He pushed my chair away from the table; the ease with which he did it showed there was definitely a great deal of strength in that sexy body. I shivered again with a mixture of fear and lust and he straddled himself on my lap, reaching behind my head with one hand and pulling me against his mouth once more. He slipped the other hand down and started to softly knead my cock through the leather. My hands were trapped because the chain between them didn't allow me to reach around him, so I settled for gently running them up and down his sides, feeling his powerful frame under his loose shirt. He seemed to quiver each time the chains bumped against him.

He eventually pulled away from my mouth and then leaned forward even further, until I felt his chin brush against my ear. His soft voice filled my ear. The words were like a velvet poison that shorted out my mind, making it impossible to think. "You're mine. I can do whatever I want to you, and you can't stop me. Your entire life is in my control."

He finished this declaration by gently tweaking my nipples, causing me to gasp again. And then he gave a little laugh, and it was like this -- all the insane shrieks and evil yells of every villain, every single mad person's shouted laughter as they plunged blades into the bellies of their victims -- they were all like the giggles of babies compared to this soft little chuckle. The room's temperature seemed to drop. This surprised me, because I was sure I had descended into hell.

I tried to move into a more comfortable position. Leather creaked and chains clinked. After that heart-stopping laugh, he unlocked the chain from my collar and told me to follow him. There was an unspoken sentence -- "You will do what I say; one way is the easy way, the other is much, much harder." My suspicions were confirmed when, after we left the dining room, the mountain of human muscle fell into position behind us. The expression 'trapped between a rock and a hard place' popped into my mind as I walked behind Tommy with my chains clinking accompanied by the heavy breathing of the muscled hunk behind me. I was very happy for this current arrangement because I felt that while the guy behind me could break every bone in my body, Tommy could steal my very soul.

We had come back to the dungeon. The muscle man waited outside. Tommy walked over and unlocked the manacles from my wrists and then handed me the key and told me to do the same with my ankles. While I was bent over, he walked over to some built-in cupboards on the far wall. He opened them, rummaged around inside them, then walked back over toward me with a grin on his face and an armful of leather and chains. He told me to strip out of the shorts I was in, and I did so. He then told me to bend over. I bent over and relaxed, and soon felt him rub a slimy finger against my asshole. I shivered, and my cock, which had been at half mast, sprang to full attention. I heard him make a noise of approval. He seemed to be turned on by the fact I was turned on.

I felt something cold and metallic press against my hole. I had to relax and stop my hole from trying to clench shut from the sensation. Again, with a tenderness that I had not anticipated, he gently worked the plug into me. There was a brief moment of pain as the widest part passed my sphincter, but then I felt my ass clench around the thin base and relax slightly. Tommy pulled me upright and turned me around. He handed me a pair of heavy leather pants, which I managed to struggle into. There were 'D' rings running up the inside and outside of each leg, as well as lacing and straps to help tighten the jeans. Tommy had me stand slightly spread-legged while he tightened the straps and lacing on each leg. The pants had fit comfortably when I pulled them on; now they hugged each leg tightly. He then handed me a pair of engineer boots and a pair of thick socks. I sat on the floor and pulled these on. This was all done in silence, but his eyes never stopped watching my every movement. The expression on his face would be best described as 'hungry.'

When I stood up, he handed me a jacket. The zipper ran up it diagonally and there were five pairs of 'D' rings on both sides of the zipper. Also, a zip around the bottom meant that the jacket and pants could be joined to form a one-piece suit. Tommy zipped the bottom of the jacket to the pants, then fiddled with a clip on the shoulder of the jacket and all of a sudden pulled the sleeve down from the shoulder. Apparently, it was a long-sleeved, doubled up and clipped to the shoulder. He joined each pair of 'D' rings traveling the length of the zipper on the front with padlocks and then had me cross my arms. I realized it was a strait jacket.

He pulled my arms tight and secured them behind me. I had been so busy looking at the zipper that I hadn't noticed that there were also a number of 'D' rings running up either side of the jacket. Tommy then held a large gag up to my mouth. I opened my mouth and he buckled it around my head. There was a large wedge of rubber filling my mouth, but when I poked at it with my tongue, I noticed a hole in the middle. While I was busy figuring this out, Tommy led me over to the center of the room where my former cell buddy had been hanging.

I looked up at the roof. There were a number of points

on the ceiling to which things could be attached, also a number of winches. Tommy grabbed a remote unit dangling nearby and pushed a button. At least six winches started to lower their cables. I had to admit, this was a very well set-up dungeon, which no doubt would have come at a considerable cost to Tommy. Then again, when you're a mob boss, I don't think money is really an issue. It may not buy happiness but it can buy fun times.

Tommy lowered the cables until one pair was at shoulder height, one at waist, and the last pair on the floor. He attached them to certain 'D' rings on the pants and jacket and then started to raise the cables again. He raised the pair attached to my shoulders first. I felt myself lifted to my tip toes. Then he raised the ones attached to my ankles. I felt a brief moment of panic as I was tipped back and my feet left the floor.

He raised the legs higher, but gave the shoulders and waist some more slack, so that when I finally leveled out I was at about waist height on him. He looked over his work with that same hungry look. He was rubbing his crotch, and through the tight leather I could make out a *very* large bulge. I hoped that this plug would do its work, or else I would be in for a lot of pain later. He moved off to the side and came back with a posture collar. He told me to look straight up, and then he buckled it around my neck. Once in place, I couldn't move my neck left or right. I had a reasonable field of view, since I wasn't all that high off the floor. I heard him move over to the side again, and he reappeared, standing directly behind my head.

He was hooking something onto the two cables suspending me by my shoulders. It was a small box with a few dials and knobs on it suspended in the middle of the two cables. It was swinging above my neck area. Tommy was gone for a while and I thought maybe he had finished; however, he reappeared soon with what looked like the bag from one of those camelback backpacks. This one had two thin, long tubes coming out of it, though, instead of one. He rested the pack on my chest and then fiddled with the tube, somehow feeding them through the small box suspended from the two cables. The end result was that the two tubes ran through the small box and then finally ended up resting against my gag.

Tommy pushed the tubes into the hole in the gag and then moved out of my field of vision again. He reappeared down near my ankles. I couldn't really lift my head much to see what the fuck he was doing, but I felt him spread my legs and then felt him doing something with my ankles. Eventually, he finished and moved off again, but I couldn't move my legs back together, so I am guessing there was a spreader bar down there.

Once again, he appeared down in my leg area, except that now he was at my crotch. I felt him fiddle around and I swung a little and then felt cool air hit my groin. I then felt cool air also on my ass. I hadn't realized the zipper was an all-around one. I felt something cold press against the back of my balls and then something cold against the front of them as well. I decided this was probably a locking ball weight, the kind you can only take on and off with an Allan key. I felt something go around the base of my penis and then on the top as well. Then I I felt it tighten, and felt my cock throb fatter in response -- probably a strap acting as a cock ring.

The next sensation was a little weird -- I felt something cool and slimy at my piss slit, and then a weird sort of 'I'm peeing' sensation. It burned a little, but not a hell of a lot; I figured it was a sound. Then I felt that he was pressing against the inside of my left leg, except that each time he pressed against my leg I also felt my cock move. I tried to lift my head, but it was no use; the collar prevented me from getting a look.

I felt Tommy press against my ankle and then heard him moving some stuff around on the floor. Suddenly he reappeared back at my crotch and I felt him fiddling with the plug and the ball weights. Then he held up something for me to see -- it looked like a small metal egg on some wires. I wondered if he was going to take the plug out and put that up there instead. Instead, he lowered it and I felt a slight tug on my balls -- it must be a weight. It wasn't very heavy, though no doubt I would begin to feel it in a few hours.

Suddenly he was back at my head. "Hey there, Mike, hope you're having fun." He turned on his 6000-watt smile again. " -- 'cause I sure am! Now let me explain this little set-up to you." At this point, he stopped and pointed toward the small box with the tubes running through it. "This is an interesting little device. It will pump one of the two liquids in the bag through the tubes. It has a randomizing function. Now, since there are only two tubes, that should give you an even 50/50 split, but ya never know. The liquids in the bag are Gatorade on one side and my piss on the other, so you will never know which one you are going to get a mouthful of. When I switch it on, it will pump for twenty seconds every two minutes of one or the other. That equals about a mouthful of fluid."

"This brings us to the next feature of your bondage. I have catheterized you." This explained the funny sensation of him pressing against my leg and the feeling traveling to my cock; he must have been taping the tube to the leg of my pants. "The end of the tube ends over a bowl, which is sitting on top of a pressure switch. Once the piss level rises high enough, it will activate the switch, which will then turn on a randomizing function to a tens unit." Oh shit, not more electricity.

"This will then deliver shocks of varying power at various times to the conductors around your balls and up your ass. The small metal object I showed you works like a plumb bob. It points straight down. It also has a motion detector in it. If it is disturbed, you will receive a very heavy shock to your balls and ass once every twenty seconds for as long as the weight is in motion. This means that for a while, the worst you will have to endure is the taste of my urine in your mouth, but soon you will receive random shocks. If one of those shocks is heavy enough and surprises you and you twitch, that will set the weight in motion. Of course, if you manage to remain still, you will only receive the occasional shock when the randomizing function kicks in. Enjoy." He disappeared from my view and I heard the door to the dungeon open and then close.

I had no idea how much time passed. I tried keeping tabs on the time by counting the number of times the unit gave me a mouthful of liquid, but I counted the intervals at one point and it was definitely not once every two minutes. I think it was on a randomizing time function to fuck with my head. It would give a little beep and I would feel liquid enter my mouth. When it was Gatorade, I would keep it in my mouth to swish it around and try to get the taste of cold piss out of my mouth. The next three cycles, however, might be piss.

I tensed up as I felt a slight buzz in my balls. Tommy forgot to tell me that the randomizer of the tens unit sometimes only sends a zap to either my balls or ass, not always both. The first one caught me completely unaware. I had just sorta zoned out by that stage, swallowing quickly whenever the pump turned on, so I didn't really get a chance to taste whatever my mouth ended up with. I had been sort of awake, dreaming. The feeling of floating like that was very peaceful. The pants and jacket were very thick, so I was a little warm . The stress made me sweat a little more, but it was nowhere near as hot as the previous night, and I had my head free.

Anyway, I had not been ready for a sudden tingle in my nuts, which surprised me so much I twitched and then regretted it. The zap my cock and ass got was lethal! I screamed into my gag and thrashed around; this, of course, was counter-productive. I nearly choked on the next mouthful of liquid and then was trying to cough with the gag in while still being zapped. Eventually, I managed to tense up my whole body and ride out the fucking zaps until they stopped. I was sweating heavily after that. I found that I tensed up when I got a zap, and then I'd concentrate on veeeeery slowly relaxing my body from my feet up.

I hadn't noticed when Tommy eventually reappeared next to me. I had been there with my eyes squeezed shut and my body tensed. I could feel my back starting to arch. I had received three sharp shocks to my nuts in about a minute and three mouthfuls of liquid in the past two or so -- one Gatorade in-between two mouthfuls of piss. When everything stopped and I finally managed to relax and open my eyes, I nearly jerked in shock, which would've undone all the hard work I had just put into not moving. He stood right there next to me smiling that smile of his.

I moaned at him through the gag. He simply laughed. "Had enough yet, slut?" I nodded carefully. He moved forward, wiped my sweating forehead and then rested his hand on my chin. "Now, how can I resist those eyes? Besides, it's getting late and I need someone to help me keep my bed warm."

He switched off the machine, reached down and switched off the tens unit. He unscrewed the ball weights, but left the plug in place and just zipped the pants closed. He grabbed the remote and lowered me to the floor. I had a little trouble standing. My legs were really weak. He didn't remove anything else, though, and once he had unattached the cables, he led me outside into the corridor.

We eventually came to a door that opened to reveal a huge bedroom -- a massive bed in the center of the room. Above the headboard was a massive sword; if I hadn't seen the size of the bulge in his pants, I might have thought he was trying to overcompensate.

While I was busy looking around the room, Tommy was busy undoing my arms. I was surprised when I found I could move my arms. I immediately stretched them out. While I was doing this, Tommy unlocked all the 'D' ring pairs and unzipped the jacket. I shivered as cool air hit my hot skin, and then he slid a hand in and tweaked my nipples. I gasped again, as it felt like another small electric shock. He moved forward and unstrapped the gag with one hand and kept playing with my nipples with the other. He pulled the gag out and I immediately started to stretch my mouth.

Suddenly, his was over mine. he was pulling me hard against him and one hand was behind my head holding me against his mouth. I had no objections. I shrugged the jacket off. It was still zippered to the pants, so it just hung off the back of the jeans. I grabbed him and pulled him against me. He growled in approval, pulled off my mouth and bit down hard on my neck. I arched my back and groaned, it felt so fucking good.

He unzipped the fly of the jeans and threw me down on the bed. He managed to get out of his tight jeans with surprising speed. His cock was a rock-hard poker sticking straight out, and there was an assured ass pounding in my near future. He sat down on my face and I rimmed his hairless hole while he groaned and unlaced the legs of my jeans. Eventually he managed to yank them off. He reached over to the side table and grabbed a bottle of lube and fully flipped me over and yanked the plug out. I let out a groan of pain and lust. At that, he grabbed the back of my hair and growled in my ear, "I'm gonna make you my bitch, and you're gonna like it, slut. Now scream for me." He then slammed his cock into me up to the hilt, and scream I did. About ten minutes later, my cries of pain became moans of pleasure, so he grabbed the back of my hair again and yanked my head back and bit down on my neck until I was yelling in agony again.

When he eventually violently orgasmed, I was spent. My back was covered in scratches, some of which were bleeding. My neck was red and felt like I had been whacked with a strap. My ass was a combination of searing pain and unbelievable horny sensation.

He lay beside me and kissed me tenderly. I was completely spent, even though I hadn't cum. He pulled the covers over us and pulled me against him and I just drifted off to sleep like that.

I woke the next morning to a stinging sensation on my back. I tried to roll over, but I was being straddled. Someone whacked my butt. "Lie still." I stopped moving at Tommy's command and instead turned my head to see what was going on. He was dabbing the scratches on my back with some ointment. Judging from the stinging, it was an antiseptic. "Got a little carried away there. Sorry, Mike, not really used to guys responding. In most cases, I would have had them restrained while I fucked them. Some just lie there, but you're the first to fully get into it."

He grinned and I felt my cock stir. Fuck, he could turn me on like a light bulb. I lay back down and tried to ignore the stinging on my back as he continued to dab the scratches with the ointment.

When he had finished, he told me to get up for breakfast. I climbed out of bed. He pointed to a chair where there was some clothing. He himself was in loose, long pants and no shirt. His body was sooo damn hot.

I grabbed the clothes. They were the leather shorts that laced up the side again. I pulled them on and picked up the other items. There was a bracelet which had two fine chains running from it to a ring. I slipped the bracelet on and slipped the ring over my middle finger. Also there was a harness made of really fine chains; apparently Tommy had a thing for metal. I slipped this over my head and settled it about myself and walked over to where he was waiting at the door. He pulled me into rough kiss, which caused my cock to grow in my leather shorts.

He led me to the dining room and I sat across from him again and we chatted. It was almost normal. I was still fairly nervous around him, but also sorta wanted to get to know him. He had a very confident manner; of course, when you considered the power he wielded as a mob boss, it wasn't surprising. He also had that justified arrogance, that look in his eye and the slight turn of his mouth. He was hot and he knew it. A lot of people find that off-putting; however, since I am shallow, I find it a turn-on. As they say, sluts have more fun.

After a while he looked at his watch. "Well, we'd better get you ready for your next trip, Mike." I was immediately on my guard again and my pulse jumped to a rate which would have led anyone monitoring it to believe I had just been given a huge fright.

"W-where am I going?" I was suddenly aware more of the fact that this was a mob boss; images of pig farms and shallow graves were flashing thought my mind.

He smiled his lazy grin. "We're heading out to my country office for a few weeks. I head out there to relax, unwind and escape the prying eyes of the vice-squad and various other specialized police units. Let's go get you packed for the trip." Somehow, his last sentence didn't quite sound right. It almost sounded as if….

I looked down at the box. It was about eight feet long and three feet wide. The inside was padded with leather. There were various straps attached to the bottom at regular intervals. I tried to keep the word coffin from creeping into my mind as I examined its other kink attachments that would obviously not be put there if the intended purpose was to merely aid in the transport of a corpse. There were 'O' rings all along the side at about one-inch intervals running up and down either side. They stopped about a foot-and-a-half from the top, and there were grooves in the wood at that end.

Tommy had gotten me to strip out of my chain, harness, and leather shorts. He handed me a pair of rubber shorts with a front-to-back zipper. I pulled them on easily because they were well-lubed. He had undone the zipper at the front and now pulled my cock out through the opening. At his touch, it immediately started to grow and I realized I hadn't cum since about two days ago, although it felt like much longer.

He strapped a leather cock ring around the base of my cock and balls and pushed them back into the rubber prison, which he zipped closed. Then he grabbed a bottle of something and squeezed whatever was in it onto his hands. He then started to rub it all over me. It was wet and slimy; I assumed it was lube. I closed my eyes and felt my cock grow even harder in its prison as he ran his powerful hands all over me. After he had lubed me all over, he grabbed a larger rubber item and squeezed lube into it as well. Then he handed it to me.

I saw it was a cat suit. Entry was through the back. I managed to struggle into it. It was a tight fit, so it was not easy to do, even though I was slimy with lube. As soon as it was on, I was already building up a sweat from the effort of getting into it. I found this easy to forget, though, because Tommy was running his hands over my body to smooth out the rubber. Once again, my cock throbbed painfully hard. Tommy then grabbed a large leather sleep sack and dumped it into the bottom of the box and told me to get in it. This was going to be one very sweaty trip.

I climbed in. There were sleeves for my arms to go into and I slid my hands into them. The leather smelled really great and felt cool against my rubbered body, although I knew it would not be cool for long. Tommy immediately zipped up the sack, then started to lace up the string over the zip, starting from the feet and working upward. This took a long time and I was already starting to heat up by the time he finished. It was very tight and I couldn't really move, although I could sort of rock my body from side to side. Tommy quickly stopped this by using the straps on the bottom of the box to strap me into place. He pulled each of them tight and even through the thick leather of the sack, I could feel them tightly holding me in place. Tommy still didn't seem to be satisfied, because he disappeared and reappeared not long after holding armfuls of rope. He threaded the rope through every second 'O' ring on the side of the box, webbing me into place. Once this was done, I tried to wiggle. I could not move an inch. People say this a lot, but I might as well have been poured in cement; I had no mobility whatsoever.

Tommy walked up to the end where my head was and then held up a piece of wood. It was rectangular in shape, but with a semi-circle cut out of one side. I didn't have to be psychic to know what was going to happen next. Sure enough, the piece of wood slid smoothly into the grooves on the sides of the box and the semi-circle closed over my neck. He then grabbed a bolt and a ratchet and started to secure it in place, using a bolt on either side. Even if I could somehow get out of the sleep sack by undoing the ropes and straps, both on the outside, and then unlace the strings over the zip and then unzip the bag, I would not be able to free my head.

When the neck piece was secured, he placed a thin, square leather pillow on my right side against the wall of the box. It was about an inch thick and rigid. He then placed one on my left. He continued this until my head was firmly wedged between two leather pillows. I couldn't shake my head, and the neck piece prevented me from lifting my head.

He then placed a small anesthesia mask over my mouth and nose. The only opening was a small hole. He pressed it firmly against my face, and then, looking deep into my eyes, he put his thumb over the hole. I had anticipated this and had managed to take a breath before he did it. I looked up into his green eyes and tried to remain calm.

Soon the pressure was too much and I released the breath and tried to draw another -- but nothing. I managed to get half a mouthful of air that must have been in the mask, but not a full lungful. The small mouthful of air only made the lack of air more apparent, and then my body's self defense kicked in. I tried to shake my head, but soft unyielding leather on either side stopped this. I was trying to thrash around, but my body was securely tied. I tried to yell, but no air was in my lungs to yell with. I felt my mind go hazy with panic, then saw spots start to appear before my eyes. This all seemed to take years. I was just feeling myself begin to float when suddenly there was air. My lungs took in a great, deep, greedy breath, and suddenly there was a taint, an almost sweet smell.... Oh fuck, he was a bastard.

When I awakened, my box had been sitting on the floor of a new dungeon. I remember thinking in my drugged haze of a mind that more then one playroom was just greedy. I had been freed of all my restraints and rubbers. I was naked. I had struggled to sit up, and a boot had suddenly planted itself between my legs. Then a strong hand in a leather glove hand grabbed my arm and I had been pulled up into a kiss. I had briefly glanced into fiery green eyes before I had closed my eyes to enjoy the sensation of a wet tongue dominating my mouth.

That had been a week and a half ago.

I stretched out and tried to scratch my groin. This activity was hindered somewhat by the chastity belt I was locked in. I sighed with frustration and put down the book I had been reading, got up and walked around a little to see if the friction of the belt against my skin would take care of the itch; it did. I wandered over to the window and looked out.

Tommy had left about five days ago and said he would be back tonight. When he left, he had locked me in the belt. I had to admit, it was a fine piece of bondage equipment that at any other time I would have admired and drooled saliva and pre-cum over. It was simple enough -- a metal tube contained my cock, and curved back toward my ass. A plate covered the ass and it was kept in place by a belt around my waist. That's where the simplicity ended; there were no locks. It was all controlled by electromagnetic locks, the codes of which could be transmitted over a cell phone that had been modified for this purpose. As a result, I had to keep my phone nearby and charged at all times. If I moved more than ten meters from my phone, I got a warning tingle in my nuts. If I moved more than fifteen meters, I got a very nasty zap on the area between my balls and ass. Reach down and pinch that area, and you would find it is a little sensitive.

The belt itself needed charging as well. When the battery got to a certain level, I got three short tingles to my balls. If I didn't get to a charger within an hour, I got a sharp zap, which then continued until the charger was plugged in or until the battery went dead.

I had tried one time. I found out my resistance died long before the battery did. There was also a special butt plug. I had to text message Tommy if I wanted to use the toilet for solid waste purposes, and he would send the code to open the plate covering my ass. Similarly, he could tell me to put the plug in and then lock the plate on, keeping it in me. If I tried to close the plate without the plug in place, it transmitted this info to Tommy. Did I mention he could also activate the voltage from his phone?

I saw a cloud of dust in the distance. My heart did a little bit of a somersault -- the usual mixture of fear and lust.

Tommy walked in and I was there to meet him. He walked over and grabbed me and kissed me roughly. When he had finished, I was in a fair bit of pain because my cock was trying to grow in its confinement. He growled at the back of his throat, "Fuck, I've been missing that, slut. Get to the playroom. I'll be along shortly."

I headed toward the playroom. The house is like an oasis in the middle of a desert; actually, it is literally an oasis in the middle of a desert. There is nothing but red, parched sand for hours in either direction. Tommy doesn't even bother pretending to farm anything out here.

It's a prison/fortress. There is a chopper kept fuelled and ready out the back, the glass is all bullet-proof, and the whole house is reinforced. That's the fortress; as for the prison, all communications can be monitored through Tommy's personal computer in his study -- phone lines, Internet, everything. The logs from my chastity belt mobile phone even get recorded on there.

To put it bluntly, I was a 'guest' until such time as Tommy chose. There was a staff of about twelve -- all huge guys. Apparently they got paid to sit around and flex their muscles while wearing tight shirts and singlets, cowboy boots and hats. It was either eye candy for Tommy or torment for me. The sight of those bulging jeans trying desperately to contain packages of leviathan proportions made my cock try to grow painfully in its confinement. No one tried to hit on me, and I ignored them as best I could. As cute as I am, I very much doubt I could seduce one to risk his life for my freedom.

I walked into the playroom and stripped off the clothes I had been wearing over my belt. I stood there in the middle of the room and waited. About ten minutes later, Tommy strolled in. He was dressed in faded jeans and old, well-worn, brown leather boots. A button-up cotton shirt and wide-brimmed cowboy hat in his hand, he looked fucking hot as hell. He pointed over to the corner of the room and I walked over there.

He had grabbed the remote for the winch system. The winch system in this play room was even more intricate. The cables not only went from floor to ceiling but four of them were on tracks that went from one end of the room to the other. One set of these was resting in the corner I was walking toward; their cables were slowly unwinding down. They reached hip height and stopped. Then Tommy walked over. He had an armful of gear. He dumped it on the floor and reached into the back pockets of his jeans and pulled out his phone.

I tensed, expecting a zap, but instead I heard the locks click open. I wasted no time in pulling the damn thing off, and in the cool air, my cock sprang to full hard-on position, something it had not been able to do for five days. I knew better than to reach for my cock, and Tommy growled in approval, then reached down and handed me something from the pile.

It was a bondage belt. I strapped it on above my naked hips and clinched it tight. Tommy walked up and slipped a lock through the specially-designed buckle. I could smell him; he hadn't showered from the trip and there was a strong masculine body odor mixed with that 'old clothes' smell from his well-worn riding gear. I shivered and my cock grew harder. He completely ignored it; instead, he attached a parachute harness around my nuts. I winced a little as he tugged my nuts roughly into place. He then stepped over to the two cables with an item from the pile of the gear.

It was a wide piece of leather. It tapered off at the ends and ended with an 'O' ring on either side. He attached the ends to the cables. Basically, it was a swing seat. He motioned for me to hop on and directed me to do it so that I was facing the closest wall. He used some chains to secure me in the seat by attaching them to points on the belt and then to the 'O' rings at the end of the seat. Basically, I couldn't hop out of the swing seat.

I was holding the cables to keep my balance. He grabbed some locking wrist restraints and buckled them around my wrists and locked them, then took some chain and attached them to the restraints, then to the cables using padlocks. He then placed a heavy collar around my neck and locked that in place as well. This had 'D' rings at regular intervals. He took some thin chains and locked them onto rinds on either side of my neck, then padlocked the other end of the chains to the restraints. Basically, I had enough slack that I could move my hands up and down the cables but I couldn't reach below waist level. I could also stretch my hand away from the cables about a foot or so. Tommy then knelt down and buckled ankle restraints around my ankles and then hooked some cord from the ankles to the back of my bondage belts.

My legs were curled up off the floor. I tried to stretch my legs and found that a bit of the cords were elastic but didn't have much give. Tommy stood and watched me kick and move around, finding the limits to my movement in my swing seat. He then walked over to the wall and secured one end of a long rope to it somehow. There must have been an anchor point there. He then walked back. This end of the rope ended in a small metal hook. He grabbed the dangling chain of the parachute harness and hooked it on.

He then stood up and smiled. "Well, Mike, there are five meters of rope here, and it's six meters from here to the remote. When I leave, this winch is automatically going to move towards the opposite side of the room. If you press the yellow button on the remote when you can reach it, the winch will stop and move back to this wall until it gets back to this position. Then it will start over. One of the buttons will stop it, of course, but you don't know which, and you don't know what the others will do. So I would advise against trying, unless you wish to possibly end up with no balls. Well, I am off for a ride. Have fun." As he left the room, the winch began to move very slowly.

I watched the elastic rope begin to uncoil. This was going to be interesting.

Four hours later, Tommy came and rescued me from my torture seat. By that stage, my balls were aching and I was exhausted from trying to stretch and grab the remote as soon as I was in reach. He took me to the bedroom and fucked me hard and mercilessly. He then rolled me over and kissed me while I gazed at him through the tears in my eyes. Then he stroked me off to a shuddering orgasm. He hugged me tight against him until we both fell asleep.

I finally worked up the courage the next morning at breakfast to ask the question. "So, how long do you usually keep a lad, sir?"

He looked up and smiled at me. "Generally, just a few days or so, but in your case, a lot longer."

It took me a few seconds to realize that he didn't mean that he would keep me for just a few weeks. I looked up. He was watching me, all traces of the smile gone. Suddenly, the room seemed very small. "W-what do you mean?" I stuttered.

He leaned back and continued to look at me. "I'd be the first person to say I am not the type to fall for guys, but I like you, Mike. You are submissive. I know I have power over you. I have seen how you go when I so much as look at you. I like having power over people, and, to some degree, I like to hurt people."

He leaned forward and I leaned back. Suddenly, the kitten was a tiger again, and I was in the tiger cage, minus a whip and chair. "That's how I got here. I can see you're scared of me, but I also know I turn you on. Most people I just scare. I hate to sound weak, but I didn't realize I missed seeing someone who knows me, look at me and be turned on. Until I met you, that is."

He got up and walked over to a side table and came back with a manila envelope. He placed it in front of me and moved behind me. "Open it." I managed to get the envelope opened with trembling fingers. It slipped from my grasp and the contents spilled across the table.

My heart froze. Time seemed to slow down. Across the table were photos -- photos of my friends, my family, a few were even of guys I had slept with. I reached out and tried to pick up one of my sister, but my hand was shaking too badly.

I think Tommy was speaking in my ear, but his voice sounded a long way off. "You see, Mike, if I just tell you you're mine and try and chain you up, you will try to escape. Maybe the fear I inspire in you will be enough to keep you from trying for a while, but after a few months, the idea of freedom will be like water to a man in a desert. This, however -- "

He reached over and pulled a group of photos closer to me. They had obviously been taken without the people knowing, because everyone was looking very casual. There was a picture of one of my good friends sitting at a table with a bunch of people at a café, laughing. " -- THESE chains are ones which you will never try to shake off. To be safe, however, I will be moving my base of operations out here. It's too easy for the police to monitor me in the city. Lately, they have been gathering a little bit too much evidence for my liking."

I felt him move away from my chair and he seated himself opposite me. Again, he looked at me. I was still frozen. I couldn't believe what I had just heard. I couldn't believe he had just casually told me, in his own way, that the lives of my friends and family depended on me staying here to be his slave slut. He smiled. "You will grow to love it, Mike. I have too much power over you for you to resist me." Deep down, I knew he was right, but at this moment I could only feel raw hatred sloshing within me.

This happened nearly a year ago. He has kept me writing normal correspondence with everyone I know, closely monitoring my emails and phone calls. However, I managed to write this story and keep it hidden from him. The lives of my friends and family depend on my caution.

He is away again, and his system is glitched on his computer slightly. It's not recording attached files. He thinks I don't know and I pretend not to.

Enclosed with this story is the evidence off his own computer needed to bring him down. The police won't move against him on a simple kidnapping charge, but with these, they will.

Help me, guys. You're my only chance. Get these files to the cops, feds, national parks, whoever!!!! Just help me!!!! I can't email them directly, so I am posting them here. I only dare try this once. Fuck, I only have one chance at it, anyway.

Attached file: 'shipping-portfolio'   *error file corrupted*
Attached file: 'bank-statements-05-06' *error file corrupted*
Attached file: 'inventory-report-weaponry' *error file corrupted*

PUBLISHER'S NOTE
Naturally, we were alarmed by this story, wanted to help him and therefore attempted to download the files. Unfortunately, they were corrupted.

HIPPY BUSTER

The young man stirred and groaned as he opened his eyes. He tried to move and found that he couldn't. His eyes opened wide in horror. He tried to move his head to see where he was, but found he couldn't do that, either. His only clue was a featureless white ceiling.

Suddenly, a familiar voice sounded nearby. "Ah, you're awake, Mr. Douglas. No doubt you're also wondering where you are." His view suddenly started to change as the top half of the bench he was on tilted up. He found himself facing a very famil-iar face.

Tony Collins was a very successful business man. He designed large office buildings for a living. He smiled at the immobile young man before him and spoke again. "Well, Mr. Douglas, or shall I call you Nick? It seems that we meet again. Last time was at the court hearing to present your case to declare a national park the area on which I plan soon to start building construction. And the time before that was when you and those other backward people you hang with chained yourselves to my bulldozers, was it not? I can tolerate you doing illegal and rather useless things like chaining yourself to machinery, but your suc-cessful lobbying crossed the line, I'm afraid."

He had been sitting down, but now stood. "I'm afraid I won't be able to see all of what is done to you, but the finished product shall be most pleasing to me. I'm afraid this is the last time I will see you face to, um, face -- although not the last time you will see me. Oh no, you can be sure of that." He then walked out of Nick's field of vision, and a moment later, Nick heard a door close.

Nick started to feel panic build up inside him; what was Mr. Collins talking about? Where was he? The man had not so much as even looked him in the eye until this point, let alone threaten him. He tried to move again and found that he couldn't. None of his body seemed to want to respond; in fact, his entire body felt heavy as lead.

He tried to remember what he could. He had been at home, preparing for another court hearing to stop the construction of Mr. Collins' buildings. He remembered hearing noise outside, in back of his house. He had gone to check it out, thinking his girlfriend Susan had locked herself out again, and then -- nothing.

A fresh wave of panic set in -- what if Susan was somewhere being held by that nut? Before his panic could progress further, his attention was brought back to his present situation by the sound of the door opening and closing again, followed by footsteps; what stepped into his field of vision next was not what he was expecting.

The man who stepped in front of him was tall, young, and in good shape. Of this, there was no doubt. His clothing was black and shiny and it hugged his body as though it had been painted on. Light played across its reflective surface each time he moved. The only area that was not perfectly outlined was the groin, where there was a large black bulge, like a sports cup; it seemed to be made of the same material, but thicker and more rigid somehow. The outfit seemed to be a combination of pants and top. The man's well-toned legs were hugged by shiny black boots that ended just below his knees. The top part of the outfit was sleeveless, but he had on long black gloves that seemed to be made of the same material that ended just above the elbows. His face was young and handsome and he had short, spiky red hair.

Nick suddenly realized that he had been standing there silent while Nick had been examining him. When his gaze met the young man's eyes, the man smiled and began to speak. "Well, patient #203, how are you feeling? The drug you were given wears off in stages. In case you're wondering why you can't move, the first stage is full immobility and unconsciousness. The second stage is merely immobility. Oh, and I would use your name Nick Douglas, but I'm afraid you are dead."

He then turned, and the wall behind him suddenly lit up. It seemed to have a large monitor built into it. On the screen was a news report. There was no sound, but Nick's heart seemed to freeze as the camera shifted its focus slightly from the reporter silently mouthing out some words to the charred, crumpled remains of a car wrapped around a tree. The plate was briefly in focus. Nick recognized it instantly as his own.

The man stepped back in front of the screen as it went blank. His words barely registered through the haze in Nick's mind. "Yes, as you can see, you died in a car crash. Rather tragic -- the day before the final court hearing for your proposal to have Mr. Collins' latest development site listed as a national park, too. Very ironic. Oh, where are my manners? I am Doctor Michael."

Nick felt cold and stunned all over. This must be some joke, some incredibly bad joke, or some sort of horrible bad dream. The sound of Dr. Michael's voice again brought him back to the present. "Yes, it seems that you made a rather powerful enemy. Mr. Collins never makes threats or anything so crass. He simply deals with people as 'obstacles' to his construction site. He removes them. But enough of just standing here talking. I will have plenty of time to explain more to you while we proceed with your, um, how shall I say, removal? Oh, and in case you're worried, Mr. Douglas, Mr. Collins does not wish you killed. Oh no; in fact, he wants you to live a very healthy, long life -- for reflection, as he puts it. Now -- to begin. I would have liked to get the procedure underway as soon as you arrived, but Mr. Collins insisted that you be awake for the whole thing." Michael moved forward to the young man on the bench. He loved this job very much.

Nick was straight, but that had not stopped him from being fascinated by Michael's rubber outfit. Michael adjusted his crotch cup as he moved toward the young man on the bench. The thought of what was to come excited him, and his erection was already pressing against the inside of the rubber cup. He activated the controls on the bench and it went back to the horizontal position.

On the bench, the young man's eyes were growing wide with fear. Michael activated the monitor above the table and Nick's eyes widened as he found himself looking at a bird's eye view of himself in loose 501 denim jeans and white t-shirt -- just as he had been when he was taken. His messy, light blond hair made him look a few years younger than he was and gave him a slight rascally look that the girls, no doubt, found attractive.

Michael quickly picked up a pair of blunt-end surgical scissors and proceeded to cut up the leg of the jeans and up the center of the shirt. He did this in swift movements because he did not wish the patient to panic too much; that made life difficult. He stopped cutting the shirt well below the neck and the jeans just below the crotch. He placed the scissors on a nearby stand, which contained all of the tools he would need to introduce this man to his new life.

Then he ripped the rest of the shirt open. He gazed down at the young man's chest; he was in reasonable shape, his stomach flat and his pecs slightly defined. Soft, golden fuzz covered most of his chest and led down toward his groin. Michael's dick gave a lurch in its rubber prison at the thought of where this scene would lead. He glanced into the wide eyes of his helpless victim and smiled an evil little grin as he traced a finger down the man's chest, lower and lower toward the first button of the jeans.

Nick felt panic overtake him momentarily as the bench he was on went horizontal. Then a section of the ceiling lit up to reveal a monitor. He was looking at someone lying on a black-padded bench. The top part of the head of a man was visible beside the bench.

Nick would have jumped, if he had been able to, when he realized it was him. He was dressed exactly as he had been. He had on his white T-shirt and comfy jeans and was barefoot. He was so entranced by the immobile image of himself that the sound of cutting material and the sensation of cold metal on his skin startled him. He wanted to yell out in fright, but couldn't move a single muscle.

The man quickly cut up the legs of his jeans and up the middle of his shirt and then tore the rest of his shirt off. Nick could do nothing as the doctor then ran his finger down his chest. The cool, smooth material of the gloves made him want to shiver. He realized with horror what the man's intentions were as the black-gloved fingers started to unbutton his jeans. Nick had nothing against homosexuals and had actively campaigned for more rights for gay couples in a number of rallies, but he was resolutely straight.

The last button was undone and Nick wanted to scream and yell for the man to stop as he watched on the monitor and felt, down at his waist, the gloved hand moving to the top of the jockey shorts he was wearing under his jeans. With a swift movement, the man tugged them down, and Nick felt cool air hit his private parts. His balls pulled up to his body slightly from the change in temperature. This seemed to amuse the doctor, who gave a small chuckle.

The monitor above him went blank, and suddenly he felt a cool, firm grip around his cock. He wanted to twist away. He desperately tried to force his muscles to obey him, but could do nothing. He heard the doctor speaking again. "Although the cock is called the love muscle, it is actually spongy tissue. Thus, the drug will have no effect on it."

Against his will, Nick felt himself growing hard from the cool grip. He felt the doctor's gloved hand run up and down his hardening member. The material had a slight plastic-like texture to it, and while the doc was this close, he could smell a slightly familiar odor -- not unpleasant. He realized it must be latex or rubber of some sort that the doc was wearing. He closed his eyes against the rush of pleasure he felt as the doc pulled his foreskin back and then up over his cock head again, slowly masturbating him. He could not believe that he was getting hard from some freak jerking him off while he was helpless on some bench.

Michael watched the man's eyelids flicker in pleasure as he slowly wanked him off. His dick was a fine specimen -- nine inches long, with a fat head on it. The foreskin slid easily up over the purple head and pulled down to expose the ever-sensitive glans. It seemed that the young man did not mind the touch of rubber, which was a good thing, considering what was coming.

Michael badly wanted to massage his own cock and jerk off over the helpless victim before him, which was why he had chosen this outfit. With the zip on the back of the one-piece, he could not easily get to his cock, which would mean he would have to finish up on the man before allowing himself to be distracted. He wished he had remembered to insert a plug before he had put the suit on, but he had things to do.

He grabbed the scissors again and quickly shredded the jeans and jockey shorts, then the sleeves of the shirt. The victim's eyes snapped open in surprise and Michael had no doubt he would have jumped and yelled in shock if he had not been under the drug's influence.

He grabbed some things from the stand beside him and activated the monitor again as he prepared the man for his first rubber experience. "I will need to shave you, Nick. We need you smooth for what's ahead." He covered the young man's chest and lower stomach with shaving foam, picked up a razor and began to remove the foam and the hair with it. He could have just used a hair removal cream, but this was so much better -- the victim helplessly watching while being shaved down, unable to stop him.

Nick could do nothing as the cool foam and his hair were scraped away from his body. The doc worked quickly, but carefully; Nick could only listen, bewildered as the doc kept up a running commentary. "After you are shaved, you will be fitted into a rubber suit. We took measurements while you were sleeping. Then we will place you in a test facility. We need to know how you will respond to long, shall we say, storage. By the way, in case at any point you were wondering where we are, I wouldn't bother. We are nowhere near your home area, so even if the police suspected you aren't dead, which they don't, they could search far and wide to find you, but they wouldn't."

The doc had finished his chest and was covering his left leg in the foam. "You're not the first person that Mr. Collins has had to remove, no, indeed. There is a place in Cairo, for instance, that now has a remarkably life-like mummy in the foyer." Nick's mind tried to process this as he felt the razor scrape up his left leg. Mummy? Had Tony Collins killed someone and mummified the remains? The doc had said he would not be killed, so what the hell was he going on about?

The doc finished the left leg and started his right. "Yes,

you see, it's very easy to get away with, and no one suspects him because he never actually threatens the people in any way. He simply watches the ringleader and then stages a tragic death for them, and the rest of the rabble makers simply dissolve after a little while. OK, all done -- oh, not quite."

Nick felt his insides lurch as the doc covered his crotch in foam and tugged his balls down. A wave of nausea was sent up through his stomach. With a few quick swipes, the doc removed all of Nick's pubic hair. Nick wanted to yell and curse the sick pervert. He wanted to call him a fucking faggot and demand he be let go, but he couldn't; he could only gaze up at the monitor and view his hairless body and exposed crotch.

He realized the doc was talking again. "And here, to give you a preview and to help turn you over is, heh, Nurse Betty." The doc seemed to find whatever he had said terribly amusing. Suddenly, Nick's vision was filled with black. A tower covered in rubber was beside him -- huge arms with muscles like footballs connected to broad shoulders, huge pecs and a ripped stomach, and right at Nick's face, a very obscene bulge in the pants that would not pass as a Betty in any language, especially Braille.

At the back of Nick's mind, a small thought popped up -- what did the doc mean by preview? He dragged his eyes away from the rubber-outlined cock and to the man's face, which he noticed was covered in some sort of black hood, with openings for the eyes and nose only. Who the fuck were these people? Did he really want to live through whatever was coming up?

He didn't have long to contemplate this as the doc and the giant flipped him over. His limbs were all loose and had to be arranged so they weren't at weird angles. The doc quickly shaved the backs of his legs up to his ass. Nick felt familiar, gut-wrenching horror as the doc spread his ass and he felt hands hold them apart while the doc spread foam over his ass and scraped it away again. He felt his face reddening and humiliation welled up in him at the degrading treatment. Despair was settling in like a cold lump in his chest slowly spreading, leaving him numb.

The doc looked down at the, no doubt, virginal asshole. He badly wanted to dip a rubber-covered finger in it, but he knew the drug would be wearing off in about half an hour and he wanted the victim secured in the testing facility before that happened. He looked up at the rubber-encased assistant and nodded over to a table where the suit for Nick was waiting. He then leaned over and spoke near Nick's ear. "One final area to shave, Nick, and then we can get you suited up and ready for the first day of the rest of your life."

He picked up the electric clippers and rested them gently against the hairline of Nick's head. He had no doubt that the boy's hair was his pride and joy. This would hopefully help break the boy; it's so difficult when they continue to be stubborn. Michael preferred to break his boys down naturally; sedated boys were no fun. He ran the clippers up the back of Nick's head and around the top of it, letting the hair fall down to where Nick would hopefully be able to see it out the corner of his eye. He left a patch at the front, and then with the help of the assistant, flipped Nick back over. The look of despair in the lad's eyes was just what Michael had been hoping for. He positioned the clippers at the front of the remaining tuft of hair, and with a quick swipe, it was gone. Then, with two more quick swipes, so were his eyebrows.

The alarm and horror he saw flash behind the boy's eyes were hot, and his cock ached painfully in its cup. It was already sweaty and slimy with pre-cum and he wanted to get this over with so he could jerk off.

He held the suit up for the boy to see. "Isn't it great? You will have so much fun wearing it. This is just a test one. Your special one is still being made, but this is okay for a boi's first suit -- because that's what you are now, Nick -- a boi. No identity and no control."

Nick barely heard what the doc was saying. These two freaks had made him scared and upset, naked and hairless. He felt his leg lifted. The inside of the suit was coated in something slimy and slippery. He felt his legs being engulfed in the tight coolness. He felt hands run up his legs, smoothing out the creases. The suit seemed to have no holes for his feet. His feet were encased in black rubber sock-like ends. Panic was growing in him as his waist was swallowed up by the tight, black rubber.

He felt his dick being manipulated into some sort of tube. Someone was roughly handling his balls, sending waves of nausea up through him. He felt his balls separated, and then felt a tight seal near the top of the sack. When the hands let go, his balls remained slightly stretched and separated. He was flipped over and was lying on the slimy chest area.

His arms were guided down into the black, hungry holes of the sleeves. The sleeves ended in black rubber gloves. His fingers were carefully guided into each separate finger. Then the back was pulled tight. He heard a zipper being done up and felt the suit tighten as it was zipped up. His chest was squeezed, but not hard enough to make breathing difficult.

He was flipped back over and he gazed up into the monitor. He didn't recognize the black-suited figure on the screen: bald and no eyebrows, completely covered in black rubber except for the bald head.

The doc leaned over him and smiled. "Well, we're nearly ready to take you to the testing facility, boi. One last thing -- I'm very sorry to say it, but this will be mildly uncomfortable." Nick looked up at the monitor as the doc grabbed a tube on Nick's suit at about crotch level. With a shock, Nick felt his cock being handled. Was his penis really that long, black, sheathed thing?

He was surprised to find his cock erect. When had that happened? He was sure he had gone soft once the doc had started shaving him. He realized that the end of the sheath felt a little tight at the base of his penis. It must be trapping blood in it like a cock ring, keeping him hard, although he found absolutely none of this even remotely erotic. He couldn't even control his penis state any more.

The doc was holding a long tube and touched the end of it to the end of the sheath. Suddenly, Nick's vision blurred as his eyes watered due to the sensation. Something was being slipped down his piss slit! It burned! How badly it burned! He desperately wanted to yell and scream, but could only lie there while the burning sensation went deeper and deeper inside him. Suddenly he felt it push up against something. There was a slight sensation of pain, and then the feeling that he had to piss.

The doc came back up to eye level. "Well, boi, you're now cathetered. The tubing is coated with a mild anesthetic, so the pain should soon stop. You will be drained of your piss constantly. Now, to make sure you receive substance." He grabbed Nick's jaw, pulled it down, and then brought his other hand up. In it was a long tube. Nick had a good idea of what was about to happen, and had he been able to, he would have clenched his mouth shut. The doc slid the tube in, and as soon as it hit the back of Nick's throat, he began to gag. The doc frowned down at him, and for the first time, Nick noticed the doc could look very menacing. "Now, boi, calm down and swallow this, or I will have to drug you and you will wake up with a shocking headache."

He continued to push the tubing in, and Nick managed to get his gagging under control. The doc's voice had been cold and threatening, and Nick desperately wanted to avoid being drugged. The tube suddenly had a weird lump of molded rubber around it and the doc stopped pushing once the lump was just inside his mouth. He pushed Nick's jaw back up, and Nick felt his teeth being pushed into a mold that worked like a mouth guard. The tube still continued over the side of the table a ways, but Nick couldn't see what was at the end. He was really scared now. He had to concentrate on his breathing, or else he felt like he would choke. His eyes were still teared up from his gagging, and the doc gently ran his fingers over them until all the tears were wiped off and Nick could see clearly.

The doc was smiling again, and his voice had its usual, warmer tone when he spoke again. "There we go, boi. All done. That wasn't so bad, now was it?" Nick desperately wanted to scream out that it was the worst experience of his whole life, but he couldn't. The doc then held up what looked like a giant black rubber band. It was about an inch thick. He slipped one end under Nick's chin and then brought the other end up over Nick's head. Nick realized he would not be able to open his mouth now when and if he ever got movement back.

The doc stepped back and dusted off his hands. "Well, boi, let's hood you up and wheel you out." The sentence made no sense to Nick, but it didn't sound good. The doc reached down, and when he held his hands in front of Nick's face again, he was holding a black rubber mask like the ones firemen wear -- the nose and eyes visible through a plastic visor. The tube ran down through the ventilator section, and Nick watched in terror as the doc fed more of the tubing through, bringing the mask closer and closer to his head. When it was there, he felt his bald head being lifted up. There was a brief moment of blackness as it was pulled over his head, and then he was looking up at the doc and the rubber giant through the plastic. Nick truly felt panic set in now. This was not good. He was totally trapped, and no one would be able to see he was in here. He wanted to thrash around, to rip off the hood and pull out the tubing, but he couldn't. He could only lie there and stare up through the visor.

He was shocked when the doc's voice sounded loud and clear in his ears. "Boi, there are earphones in the hood, so you can hear me. We're now ready to take you to the testing facility." He was lifted up by the rubber giant and placed in a wheelchair.

For the first time, he got a brief glimpse around the room. All around were benches with various items on them. Some were empty; those had presumably had the suit and mask resting on them. His breathing was heavy and loud in his ears as he was wheeled along a plain corridor. There were a few people around, but they ignored the three. Nick wanted to scream for help, wanted one of them to know he would do anything just to have his old life back. If he was released now, he wouldn't cause any more trouble for Tony Collins. He wouldn't even look at another bulldozer. Just please let him out.

Helpless and mute, he was pushed along until they came to a door with an 'Authorized Personnel Only' sign on it. He was wheeled through. There was a lot of activity all around. He was wheeled into a room similar to the one he had been in before, except no benches -- just a large, square black box. It was easily 2' by 2'.

Nick wondered what the fuck was going to happen next. The rubber giant walked over to the box and fiddled with something on the side. Suddenly, the front of the box swung down and the top slid back. Icy fear gripped Nick as he looked at the inside. It was basically an electric chair, except black and padded. It sat in the center, thick straps covering it. Nick knew he was going to be put in it, and he would have given anything he had ever owned, or done anything, if he could just not be strapped into that chair, for once in it, even if he got movement back, he was doomed.

The rubber giant picked him up and sat him in the chair, putting a hand against his chest to stop him from flopping forward. The doc came over, squatted down in front of Nick and grinned. He reached for something at Nick's shoulders, and Nick felt straps cross over his chest and tighten. The doc let Nick's head tilt down so Nick could watch as he and the rubber giant buckled Nick's legs in. The straps were at four-inch intervals, and then there was a pair of ski-type clips in the bottom of the box. His feet were placed in them and pressed down. He felt pressure surround his feet and half-imagined he heard them click into place. His arms were next, the doc grinning at him the whole time.

At the end of the armrests were circles with lots of tiny straps. Nick's hands were placed on these and each finger strapped down. He was truly helpless and immobile. His head was pressed back against the backrest of the chair and strapped into place. The doc gave him a small pat on the head and then squeezed in beside him to do something at the back. Nick saw his catheter tube being pulled behind him and felt his breathing and food tube pulled over his shoulder. He then felt something clip onto the left shoulder of the suit, and then there was a slight pull, as if something was attached to it.

The doc stepped back, smiled again, and gave Nick a wave. Then the top of the box was slid into place. Nick's heart raced as the front of the box was ever so slowly lifted into place. It seemed to take forever, and he thought his heart would stop when the last of the light disappeared and he was alone.

He suddenly heard the doc's voice in his ear. "Well, boi, you're nice and safe in there. We just need to see how you react to sensory deprivation and isolation, as well as bondage. Monitors are built into your suit, so we see your heart and breathing rate here. Your suit will also fill with liquid every now and again. That's to help rid you of any remaining hair, and to prevent re-growth. Soon we will be sending something into your stomach via the tube in your throat. It contains nutrients and a light sedative to help you sleep. Also, any fecal waste (or shit, in laymen's terms) in your lower colon will be liquefied and absorbed, then passed as urine. White noise will help ease you into this, boi. After we have you ready and know you can take the sensory deprivation and lack of movement, we will bring you out. And then, boi -- my dear, helpless little boi -- the real fun will begin."

Nick could only feel his mind reel in horror at the doc's words. Then he felt the tube in his mouth move, as though something was being pumped through it. Soon he fell asleep.

Nick felt like he was floating. He had no idea how much time had passed. He had tried to think of how many times he had awakened, but he couldn't remember. He suspected that he was being drugged. Occasionally he had awakened to find that the suit had filled with the odd liquid which the madman had said would be getting rid of the rest of his hair.

He felt his mind grow a little clearer. Obviously, the last batch of drugs was starting to wear off. He strained against his restraints and tried to listen or see anything, but there was nothing. He couldn't even hear his own breathing because of the built-in earplugs. Sometimes he fancied he heard a slight buzzing noise, but he wasn't sure if it was the headphones which had been silent since the maniac's last message to him or his own imagination. He struggled against the tight, impossible bindings; trying to move even a finger was impossible. He wanted to scream in frustration, curse and swear at the fuckers who had kidnapped him and put him in this hell hole. He wanted out of this fucked-up suit. He wanted to be away from these maniacs.

A man looked up from his console. "Doctor, his heart rate

is climbing again. He has been out of the drug's influence for twelve hours this time."

Doctor Michael looked up from the file he was reading a few desks over. "Very well, sedate him again. We will take him out after this. He is responding well, and Mr. Collins is eager for the next stage to continue. Have the tanks prepped and ready to go."

He got up and walked out the door and down the feature-less corridor to a room. Inside was a rubber-encased mummy, lying on the table. Every now and again it gave a twitch. Michael walked up to it, not bothering to try and walk quietly, and stroked the bound man. The encased figure jerked at the contact, then started to buck around on the table and make frantic groaning noises. Michael knew there would be more than groans had it not been for the heavy gag. He smiled and reached for a remote control on a nearby shelf. He would have plenty of time to play with his new toy for a little while before he had to go supervise Nick's final preparations for a new life.

Two days ago, Danny had been cruising the clubs. The usual ones had been out, the posers in their leather who only put out when the wallet came out -- the wannabe skins who still probably lived with their moms, the eighty-nine-year-old geriatric masters whose idea of breath control was to accidentally stand on the tubes of their respirators. He leaned back against the wall and sighed; the scene was so fake, and there wasn't another rubber boi out there to play with. That made it suck even more. He had taken care to look his best, though; he would never admit it, but he liked to pose for the lads a bit himself. He was in a dark maroon rubber shirt and black rubber 501s. His boots were 14-hole Doc Martins. He knew he was probably looking like a wannabe skin, too, but his hair was just long enough not to be classed as shorn, and he never tried to pass himself off as one, anyway.

He rubbed his crotch absentmindedly. Under the tight-fitting rubber, he wore rubber shorts with a sheath and a built-in plug. He had lubed the sheath well before heading out, and the horny sensation of his cock sliding into the slippery prison under the 501s was turning him on more then he had anticipated. He clenched his butt cheeks around the plug and felt his cock jerk in response.

He straightened up. Time to head home, strip down and jerk off with his nose buried in his rubber jeans, smelling the strong rubber scent that he knew would send him into an intense orgasm.

Just as he was about to make a beeline for the exit, however, a flash at the bar caught his eye. Well, 'flash' wasn't the word, really. 'Gleam' was more like it. Just as the name suggested, that shiny thick reflection meant only one thing -- rubber.

Danny moved, almost in a trance, to try and see who it was. His heart nearly stopped in his chest when he saw a tall young man standing at the bar, his short red hair spiked up, his black rubber shirt ending just at the waistband of his form-fitting black jeans. The only thing stopping the outfit from earning him an 'indecent exposure' fine was the black rubber cup that was attached over the top of the jeans. It was being held in place by about six pop clips and was no doubt very easy to detach.

Danny dragged his eyes away from the cup and back to the guy's face, which was now looking directly at him and smiling. The guy stepped away from the bar and walked over to Danny. "See anything you like there?" His voice was even and playful.

Danny flashed him a quick grin. "Fuck, yeah. Good to see other horny rubber bois out."

The guy laughed. "Rubber, yes. Boi, no. Wanna drink?"

Over a few drinks, Danny found out that the guy's name was Michael and that he was a recruiter for a modeling agency. Danny tried not to let the excitement show on his face. He had been trying to land a modeling job for a while now. He leaned back casually, trying to let the light shine on his well-defined body and nicely-angled face. "Wow, that must be exciting. How long ya in town for?"

Michael flashed him a quick smile and his eyes flickered quickly over Danny's body. "Not long, actually. Just here to sell an investment property I bought a few years back. Do you wanna come have a look at it?" He flashed his sly smile at Danny again and Danny returned the grin.

"Sure, why not?"

They stepped out of the club and Michael indicated a black jaguar parked near the entrance. Danny was not the type to chase sugar daddies, but Michael was looking interesting in more than a strictly sexual way. As they sped through the streets, Michael casually reached over and stroked a finger across the bulge in Danny's jeans. Through the awesome sensation, Danny heard Michael say something about getting some modeling work for him. Danny grinned as he closed his eyes and enjoyed his cock being stroked. This was getting better and better.

They arrived at the flat and entered. There wasn't much furniture around -- a few wooden crates were here and there. Danny noticed a large black bag near the table in the main area of the room. Hanging almost enticingly out of it was a long rubber sleeve, and the bulges in the bag suggested that it was stuffed very full. Could it possibly be full of rubber?

He only half-heard Michael trying to explain to him about some contract he had to sign. "Huh? Oh yeah, sure. Where do I sign?"

Michael laughed. "Hold up, now, buddy. First I need an audio file saying you're signing of your own free will and not under duress." Danny turned. What he really wanted was to get Michael naked and to explore that bag. He tried not to look impatient as Michael held up a small digital recorder for him to speak into. "Okay, umm, hi, I'm Danny Peterson, and I am under no duress to sign this document. Or whatever. Will that do?"

Michael stopped the recorder with an oddly satisfied look on his face. "Sure will. Sign here, and then we can get down to some real business."

Danny glanced at the thick document. There was only dim lighting in the room and the print was small. He didn't like going through it all. He knew there were watch dog agencies that would help him, so he flipped to the last page and scrawled his name at the bottom. "There! Now, what the fuck is in that bag?!"

Michael turned. "Oh, yeah. I forgot I left that there. Have a look." He reached into the bag and pulled out a long rubber cat suit. He held it and turned to Danny. "Wanna try it on?"

Danny reached eagerly for it, but Michael pulled it out of reach and laughed. "Jeans and boots off first. I don't want it getting caught on one of the buttons."

Danny struggled out of his 501s and boots and was reaching for the waistband of his rubber shorts to pull them off when Michael stopped him. "No, leave them and the shirt on. I wanna enjoy taking them off later. Oh -- no, wait. Lift up the shirt for a second."

Danny impatiently tugged the shirt up and felt Michael stick something over his nipples. He tried to look down, but Michael pulled the shirt back down. "Just helps bring out your nipples a little better, so you look even hotter." Danny smiled and Michael handed him the cat suit. It was already dusted with talcum inside and Danny slid his legs into it. The cool feel of the rubber sliding over his legs made his cock throb painfully in its lubed sheath. The opening was at the back, so he pulled the bottom half right up and felt his feet settle comfortably in the built-in socks. The rubber squeezed him in a way that turned him on more. He found that there was a small opening at the groin region. Michael showed him that it stretched open wide enough to let him slip his sheathed cock and balls through and then was tight enough to act as a cock ring -- not that Danny felt his cock would be getting soft at any stage. Danny slid his arms into the sleeves. They ended in mitten-like ends. The fingers were all separated like a glove, but on the outside it looked like a penguin flipper.

Since Danny's hands were now useless, Michael zipped him up at the back and showed him into the bedroom, where there was a large mirror. Danny was entranced. He ran his hands, trapped in their mitten-like ends, over his body. Michael stepped up behind him and pushed against his butt. Danny leaned back and moaned as the plug was rubbed over his prostate.

Hanging at the front was a hood. Michael gently stretched it back over Danny's hair. Danny looked again in the mirror and felt he would blow his load then and there. The hood had mouth, eyes, and nose holes.

Michael frowned. "Fuck, you would look better completely covered. Wanna try it?" He held up a hood that was to Danny the stuff of wet dreams. He rubbed his free hand against Danny's butt and pressed down on the area where the butt plug was under the layers. Danny moaned again and nodded.

Michael stretched the hood over Danny's head. This was a bit of a struggle, as it was a fairly tight hood. Danny was blind for a minute or two as Michael maneuvered the breathing tube into Danny's mouth. The tube was in the center of a gag that was like two halves of a mouth guard. Danny bit into them, and when the hood was finally on, he found that the elasticity of the hood prevented him from opening his jaw. The tube was about five inches long. There were no nose holes and the eyes were covered in a dark plastic, which made it very hard to see anything in the dim light.

Michael was beside him and groaned, "Fuck, you look hot. Let's get you outa that and fuck."

They moved toward the bed and Danny almost fainted when he saw his most ultimate fantasy on the bed -- a sleep sack!!! He made pleading noises through the gag and pointed at the sack. Michael looked surprised. "You wanna try it? OK, no prob. Once I get you naked, I can't guarantee that I will be able to hold back. Oh, wait -- it's tight around your neck, so you will need a collar or it will pinch."

He disappeared into the other room and was back before Danny could even move. Holding a collar, he quickly buckled it around Danny's neck. It covered the cat suit's zipper and Danny thought he heard a weird click, but he realized it was probably just the noise being distorted through two layers of rubber. Michael indicated for him to lie in the sack, and he eagerly did so, sliding his hands into their rubber mittens down the internal sleeves. The rubber was thick and strong, and Michael had to pull and tug it over Danny. Danny felt the tight, unyielding embrace as the zipper was pulled slowly up, the rubber binding him tightly. Danny gave an experimental struggle to see if he could move; he couldn't. The zipper was a double zip, and with a bit of adjustment, Michael had his cock straight up out of the sack while the rest of his body was immobile.

Michael sat back and smiled. "Well, that was almost too fucking easy. You're one dumb horny boi, you know that? Do you have any idea what you signed?" Danny tried to work out what the fuck Michael was talking about.

Michael got up and came back with the document he had signed. "It was right here in the first line. All I had to do was place a catsuit in an easily-spotted place and you fell for it hook, line, and sinker. Here -- '...by signing this document, I give power-of-attorney and all control over my physical body to Doctor Michael (that, of course, being me) for a period of no less than three years and no more than five.'"

Danny's blood seemed to freeze in his veins. This wasn't funny. Why was Michael doing this? He tried to laugh through the gag -- obviously, it was some sort of joke to get him helpless and then scare him a little.

The smile that appeared on Michael's face, however, made the laugh die in his throat. "Oh, dear, you think I'm kidding? Well, you're in for a nasty surprise. You see, Danny, I work for a very powerful man with many powerful lawyers. Even if anyone does find you, that document and that audio file make any case baseless. But don't worry -- I will take good care of you, and the contract does state that you're doing this for $200,000 a year. That's not bad money, Danny, and I can assure you, you will not be in a position to withdraw from the account for a while, so the interest should be rather substantial. Now to finish you up and ship you off."

Danny's mind was spinning. All thoughts of sex were gone. His heart was beating a rapid tattoo against his ribcage.

He struggled desperately. Suddenly, all he wanted was to be out of this gear, which had gone from horny play stuff to a prison. Michael ignored his frantic struggles and went back to the other room. Danny did not notice him until Michael sat back down beside him and grabbed his cock. Danny was amazed to see his cock still rock-hard, then remembered that the tight cat suit acted as a cock ring.

Michael held a pin up, and Danny struggled with renewed vigor. Michael looked annoyed and slapped Danny's cock and balls hard, causing tears to form in Danny's eyes and a new wave of cold dread to echo through him. "Stay still, or I might miss you, and you don't want that. Didn't I say I would take care of you? Now, let's see." He again held Danny's dick, and with a swift jab, stabbed into the tip of the rubber with the pin.

Danny cried out, then realized there was no pain. Michael must have jabbed into the rubber at the piss slit, the pin hitting nothing but air. Danny glanced back down. Michael was now holding a tube to the end of his sheathed cock, and, pressing the tube, tore larger the small hole made by the pin. Danny felt the tube begin to enter his piss slit. What the fuck was going on? He yelled into the gag as best he could as the burning sensation in his dick got more intense. He felt the tube hit something inside him, followed by a weird feeling that he had to pee. He looked down. At the end of the tube was a clear hospital bag; he realized it must be a catheter.

Through his disbelief and horror, he heard Michael's voice. "The bag is just for the trip to the lab. Once there, I will connect the tube to a drain, or maybe to your gag, if you keep struggling like that."

Danny froze. He knew what would come out of the tube and he did not want it going into his mouth at any cost. Michael smiled an evil grin that froze Danny's heart again. "Much better now. One final step and then to pack you up." Danny realized that was the second time Michael had said something about packing. His mind was too clouded with fear to even begin to guess what it meant.

Michael came back, holding what looked like large rubber wheels about seven inches wide. Michael put one of them down, then lifted Danny's feet and started to move the other one around his feet. Danny saw that they were actually rubber strips, like bandages. *He was being mummified!*

Michael calmly and patiently wrapped Danny. Danny was torn between struggling and facing some terrible punishment if he moved. When Michael finished wrapping him all the way up to his neck, he reached over to the side table and picked up what looked like a TV remote. "I would have preferred to test this earlier, but it may have given the game away." He pushed something on the remote and Danny couldn't help but jerk as a slight erotic tingle traveled through each nipple and up and down the inside of his cock. A deep groan rose from the back of his throat and vibrated up the tube, causing Michael to grin. "Yes, Danny, those pads I put over your nipples earlier are connected to this, as are some wires running down the outside of the catheter tube. Now, that was rather enjoyable, I know. You should be warned, however, that it can go fairly high. I will give you a very brief example of a punishment shock to deter you from ever misbehaving. You could almost call it shock therapy." He laughed wickedly.

He pushed another button before the words and the bad joke had been able to sink into Danny's mind. Danny screamed into the gag and thrashed around as much as he could. It felt like a red hot poker had been jammed down his cock and branding irons placed against his nipples. It lasted a split second only, but Danny was left panting for breath with his heart racing.

Michael gave him a grin. "So let's be good, okay?" He

stood up and reached under the bed, pulling something out from under it. Danny heard wood being dragged across the wooden floorboards. He tried to turn his head but couldn't. He soon found out what it was, however, when Michael grabbed his mummified feet and pulled them off the bed, then moved up, grabbed his shoulders and lifted him down.

Danny saw he was in a crate. It seemed to be lined with thick rubber padding, and his mind noted that it was fairly comfy. Michael smiled down at him. "Well, this is your mode of transport to the lab. The movers are coming tomorrow. Now, I can't have you making too much noise in there bumping against the sides."

He reached down beside Danny and Danny felt large straps being fastened over him. He could not move a fraction. He could nod his head up and down a half inch if he really tried, but a wide strap over his forehead put an end to that.

Michael then produced a bottle and placed it at the end of the gag. "Now, Danny, stay calm. I am going to give you something that will put you to sleep and also soften any shit that's in your bowels, making it pass as liquid waste. Drink in gulps and don't panic. You're going to be fed this way a lot, so you had better get used to it." He also held up the remote for a split second and Danny understood the silent threat. Trying to stay calm, he gulped the fluid down. It tasted sweet. Michael only tilted the bottle, gently pouring small mouthfuls down the tube and giving Danny plenty of time to breathe between mouthfuls. By the end of the bottle, Danny was already feeling drowsy. Michael stood up. "Well, Danny, see you back at the lab." Danny vaguely recalled the lid being lowered in place and then there was darkness for a long time.

The next day, Michael watched the muscular movers lug his crates down to the waiting van. He was dressed normally in an expensive black suit. One of the movers grunted as he and another mover carried a long narrow crate. "Geez, mister, what have you got in here? A body?"

Michael gave a laugh. "Now, why would I have a body in there?" He strolled out as they carried the last box. 'The body was in the *first* one you moved,' he thought to himself.

Michael looked down at the bucking shape. Danny had awakened a few hours ago, and Michael had fed him some more nutrient mix. A few more days, and he would take him out of this mummy outfit and dress him in a dog suit, then maybe make him a houseboi, if he was good. But for now, he pressed the button and watched the rubber shape squirm in a hypnotic gyration as the helpless victim under all the rubber came, came and came.

Soon Michael would have to get changed for the final stage for Nick. Ah, now *that* would be fun. Maybe he would tell the boi about it to put some fear into him. A little primal fear was an excellent method for training a stubborn lad. And what was going to happen to Nick was sure to make even the most demented rubber pig's blood turn to ice…

Michael sat, enjoying his moaning, wiggling rubber prisoner. He wondered what was going through the poor, dumb kid's mind. He had been so easy to trick. He had stripped down while he was playing with his slave, and now he felt like getting rubbered up. He switched the dial on the remote to a low setting -- one he knew would arouse the bound, helpless, and only vaguely human-shaped rubber package in front of him. He then turned his attention to his wide selection of rubber gear.

He grabbed his favorite rubber undies first. They had a built-in plug and sheath. He squeezed some lube down into the sheath and then onto the plug as well. He pulled them up, and then inserted the plug. He groaned quietly to himself as the plug penetrated his ass, filling him in that awesome way that only a plug can. As always, he speculated on the mindset of the first person to ever contemplate sticking such a shaped object up his ass. When the plug was fully in, and his ass clenched down tightly on the narrow base, he inserted his now-hard cock into the sheath. He shivered slightly as his penis met the cool, slimy lube. He carefully pulled and stretched the sheath so that his balls were snugly held in a separate part and the base was firmly around his cock -- not tight enough to act as a cock ring but snug enough for the wearer to be constantly aware of its presence.

He smoothed the rubber over his hard cock. The temptation to keep jerking was there, but he managed to not do so. He then pulled the undies comfortably into place. Next, he selected some long rubber socks and gloves. He pulled them on and smoothed out the rubber, his hand again straying down toward his cock. He stopped himself, as he wanted to be horny for the upcoming procedure.

He grabbed his thick, rubber shorts next. He knew that the layering would have him sweating like all hell, but he knew he would love every minute of it. Anyway, he would be too tempted to press against things to stimulate himself, and the built-in hard rubber cup would stop him from doing that. He concentrated for a few seconds on nothing in particular, running some of the less interesting business of the day through his head until his erection subsided enough for him to pull the shorts up and stuff his cock and balls into the cup. As soon as the shorts were in place, his cock sprang to attention again and was uncomfortably squashed up against the inside of the cup.

Next, he pulled on a pair of tight rubber chaps. He leaned over and zipped the inside up, loving the feeling of the rubber tightening around his legs. Then he put a pair of Doc Martins over the top. He did have rubber boots, but nothing could beat the look of a pair of 20-hole Docs over the tops of rubber chaps.

His lower half done, he pulled a simple rubber short-sleeved 'T' over the top of his head and smoothed out the wrinkles. He looked in the mirror at his reflection. His short, spiky hair made him look very sexy. He turned back to the remote and set the randomizer so that shocks would randomly be delivered to the electrodes connected to the slave in the suit. Then he turned and left the room.

Blinding light jerked Nick back into reality as the front of his prison was lowered. He tried to struggle against his bonds, but found his limbs unresponsive. Fuck, the shitheads must have sedated him again.

The front of the box lowered, and soon there was that sadistic prick in front of him smiling. Nick just wished he could get out and get his hands on that smug son-of-a-bitch.

Michael stepped up toward him and started to disconnect the tube over his shoulder. He was wearing a microphone near his mouth and Nick assumed that it was what was transmitting his voice to the receivers in his hood. "Well, Mr. Douglas, I am happy to say that you seem to be mentally adjusted to long periods of confinement. We will continue to sedate you in the upcoming weeks, of course, but gradually wean you off them."

Nick felt the straps being loosened, and when the ones over his front were released, he would have slumped forward had it not been for Michael holding him up against the chair. Michael tapped his microphone and then Nick saw his mouth moving but without sound. He realized Michael must have turned it off. Then he saw two huge men step into the room. They were in tight leather jeans and white t-shirts. They stepped up, grabbed Nick's body and held it up while Michael undid the rest of the straps, stepped around the side and appeared again with a wheelchair.

Nick was lifted up and dumped into the chair unceremoniously. Michael's voice sounded in his ear once again as he was wheeled through the corridors. "We're going to have some fun today, Mr. Douglas. Well, when I say 'we,' I mainly mean me. You're just along for the ride, really." Nick felt the familiar heavy feeling of dread and icy cold fear settle in on him. He glanced through the visor of the gasmask as he was wheeled past people. None paid any attention to him. He was beginning to doubt more and more that there would be any salvation for him.

Michael inhaled deeply as they entered the room. The room was sizable. There was the strong smell of rubber all around. People were wearing protective clothing and goggles. He glanced over to one corner and smiled -- there sat the two halves of the cylinder. Ah, if only his victim knew what was in store for him; oh well, he would know soon enough. He deactivated the microphone, knowing that Nick would not be able to hear him.

He then gave orders to the two orderlies. "Place him on the table and get the suit." They lifted the limp form of Nick onto the table; it was thick and padded in leather. Michael went over and ran his hand over Nick's rubber form. He glanced at the visor and saw the helpless eyes peering up at him. His cock twitched in its hard prison at the thought of this helpless man -- removed, thought dead by all who knew him, under his control, and soon to be isolated from the outside world forever.

He activated the microphone again. "Well, Mr. Douglas, let's get you out of that suit, shall we?" He saw the brief flicker of hope flare in the man's eyes and could not wait to see it extinguished again.

He unzipped the suit and motioned for one of the orderlies to help him. Slowly they extracted the limp form of Nick from the suit. Nick's cock sprang to life when it was exposed to the cool air and Michael could not help but take it in his hand and pump it briefly.

Nick felt hope flare up from within him again. Get him out of the suit? Maybe this would mean it was all over. He knew he would never tell a soul what had happened if they would just promise to let him go.

He was rolled over and moved about as they pulled the tight suit off him. It felt good to have his skin exposed to the cool air again. Just to be able to move again was great, even if he was unable to do it for himself. It also felt awesome to have the fucking annoying presence of the catheter removed. Knowing that the burning sensation was being caused by the fucking thing coming out as opposed to going in also made the pain almost bearable. When his cock was exposed to the cool air, it sprang up hard as all hell, and when the doc took it in his rubber-gloved hand and gave it a few pumps, Nick saw stars before his eyes. Fuck, he was fucking horny as hell. He was being held hostage and these maniacs were probably going to kill him and he was horny.

Then he realized that he had no idea how long he had been in that fucked-up box. It must have been a while because he could not remember being so horny in all his life. The cool, smooth hand rubbing his cock felt so good. He so badly wanted to cum. Then the hand stopped and he wanted to scream out in frustration.

The doc appeared in his field of vision again with that grin that Nick had come to fear so very much. "Well, it looks like someone enjoyed that! Maybe this won't be so bad for you. Now, let's get this hood off."

Nick was again momentarily blinded as the hood was

pulled off and he felt cool, sweet-smelling air wash over his face. On second thought, the air wasn't all that sweet-smelling at all; it had the scent of ammonia. Nick started to worry; the doc didn't remove the rubber band-like strap around Nick's chin and head, either, even though Nick was drugged again and unable to move. This worried Nick. He had thought that when they took the catheter out, they would also take the tube out of his throat, but this did not seem to be happening.

Michael reached over and grabbed the suit that the orderly was holding just outside of Nick's field of vision, his eyes eagerly watching the horror and fear that flickered in Nick's eyes. He watched as Nick's hopes were crushed. Michael's cock grew against its imprisonment as he squeezed down on his plug. All this control over the helpless guy was turning him on in ways he could not describe. He knew one thing for sure -- when this was all over, his helpless slave in his room would be getting one hell of a work over while Michael pumped his cock over his mummi-fied form.

Back to business, he handed the suit to the orderly. "Nice, isn't it? It has a few more features than your last model -- an upgrade, if you will. But first, if I may direct your attention over to the tanks which are the cause of that particular smell."

He gently tilted Nick's head over so that he would be able to see the large tanks and the complex machinery next to it. "You may or may not have heard of a three-dimensional printer. It fires lasers into liquid plastic to solidify it. It basically prints out a three-dimensional object layer by layer. We are doing something similar, but with rubber. You will see what it is soon enough. All you need to know is while you were in the box, some rather intimate measurements were taken. Now, back to the suit. It has built-in sensors and a few other surprises. I will explain more when you are in it."

Michael nodded to the orderlies and they again began to manhandle Nick into the tight-fitting rubber. This suit was a little thicker than the last, so it took a bit longer. Michael smiled as he saw a tear run down the side of Nick's face. As he was basically stuffed into the suit, Nick must have finally realized that all hope was gone. Michael squeezed his ass on the plug again and sighed. If this got any hotter, he felt that he would soon explode into his rubber cup.

Nick felt numb. His whole brain was just ringing with silence. He was going back into another fucking suit, and they were doing some fucked up thing with a 3-D printer, whatever the fuck that was. He felt a tear run out of his eye. This was so unbelievable. Here he was, being once again encased into a rubber suit by these fucking huge guys -- naked, hairless, gagged, and unable to move. He wanted to scream, to push them off, but he had to lie there while more and more of his body was encased and covered. The rubber was pulled and stretched to envelop his body into smooth, shiny blackness, slowly swallowing him up, all his humanity stripped away layer by layer. That sick fucking doctor was just standing their smiling while he turned another human into an object.

The doc stepped forward as the suit reached up to Nick's hips. He rolled Nick on his stomach. He quivered with excitement; he had been looking forward to this ever since Nick's limp body had been brought into the lab. He ran a finger over Nick's bubble butt and saw the skin goose-pimple up. He smiled and got one of the orderlies to hold Nick's cheeks apart. "You may enjoy this, Mr. Douglas, or you may not. I guess we won't know, since you're gagged and unable to talk."

He picked up a tube of lubricant from the table and held it above the spread cheeks. He pointed it down at the puckered, pink opening of Nick's ass. He slowly squeezed the tube, and was mesmerized as the dollop formed and then lazily dribbled down to plop onto Nick's asshole. He regretted that Nick was sedated; he would have liked to see him struggle against the orderlies, but that was not a possibility, as he might damage the suit and it was incredibly expensive. He sighed to himself as he picked up a syringe full of lube with no needle at the end and rested it against Nick's ass. It didn't matter; he'd use his con-tracted slave in a re-enactment down the track. He'd scare him into thinking the same thing that was about to happen to Nick was about to be done to him. He knew the boi would be sure to struggle rather earnestly, if he thought that was the fate that awaited him. He slowly began to press the end of the syringe against Nick's virgin ass.

Nick was snapped out of his self pity as he felt his ass cheeks spread apart. What were these sick cunts up to now? He felt nothing for a little while; then, he would have jerked, had he not been drugged, as a cool dollop of something landed on his asshole. A dark suspicion began to creep up through the layers of his brain -- surely not! Then he felt cold dread as something blunt pressed against his ass and more pressure was applied. No, this wasn't happening.

Soon, the doc would stop and say it was just something to clean Nick's ass. Other wild possible explanations flowed through Nick's mind as the pressure increased, and then a sear-ing pain like nothing he had ever felt before shot up from his ass. He wanted to scream. He wanted to arch his back and shout the walls down. This was like nothing he had felt before. The searing pain in his ass continued and spread, then withdrew, and Nick realized that he was breathing in short, sharp gasps.

He felt a funny sensation in his ass like he had something in there to shit out, but not solid like a shit. Then his heart froze up again as he felt something else rest against his ass; it was cold as ice. Nick wanted to move away from it, but began to feel the pressure increase again. Then the pain shot through him again, but this time it was much worse. Whatever was being pushed in was much thicker than the first object. He felt like a bus was being parked up his ass. He thought he would surely pass out from the pain. The object just kept getting wider and wider. He wanted so badly to scream out. His breath was rasping as he concentrated on breathing through his nose because of the fucked-up tube in his throat. Then, just as he felt for sure that he was going to pass out from the pain, the object went thin again, but he was feeling like he had to shit something out.

Michael pushed until the syringe penetrated Nick's ass. He heard Nick's breathing change and smiled. He really wanted to hear Nick groan as his virgin ass was invaded for the first time. He injected all the lube up into Nick's ass, then pulled the syringe out and grabbed the metal plug. Again he rested the tip of the plug against Nick's ass and slowly pushed down. The plug wasn't all that wide, but he knew it would feel enormous to Nick's virgin ass; he should be grateful that the muscle relaxant prevented him from clenching his ass up, or else he would really have been complaining.

Michael slipped the plug in, then nodded. The orderlies flipped Nick back over. Nick's eyes were wide and his nostrils were flared and he was breathing and sweating like he had run a marathon; his face was red and flushed. Michael couldn't help but laugh. "That's nothing. You should be grateful it wasn't a dick. Then you would really have something to complain about."

He snorted to himself again as he started to massage some life back into Nick's cock. It didn't take the treacherous organ long to betray its owner and grow hard. Michael guided it into the built-in sheath, separating the balls into their own little sack. Then it was a simple matter to pull the rest of the suit onto Nick and zip it up. This suit zipped up at the front and Michael loved the look in Nick's eyes as he pulled the zipper firmly up under Nick's throat. He grabbed the sheathed cock and slowly fed the new catheter down Nick's shaft, knowing how humiliated and angry Nick would be feeling right about now. He had basically been raped in full view of an entire room of people who had paid about as much attention as if he were waiting for a bus.

As he slid the catheter down through the slit in the sheath, he glanced over at the tank and saw a rubber form rising out of it. Good, it looked nearly complete. He finished with the catheter and then reached under the table for the truly diabolical part of the suit.

Nick was trying to deal with the invasion in his ass. His ass didn't hurt as much now, and the sensation was weird -- not exactly what he would call enjoyable, but that sorta weird pain that borders on pleasure, like when you whack your funny bone. He felt the suit hug him tightly as it was zipped up to just under his neck, then the burning invasion of the catheter. He was numb now. He knew that the brain had self-defense mechanisms, like the inability to remember actual pain. He wondered if all of this had overloaded his senses. He certainly felt numb all over.

Then the doc was holding something up for him to see -- it was about three quarters of a meter long -- molded black rubber, all twisted and warped, sort of snake-like. It tapered down to a thin point at one end and a fat, circular base at the other.

Nick couldn't care less what it was. His only relief was that all his orifices were currently filled, so at least the sick cunt wasn't going to try and shove that anywhere -- although, if Nick had been able to talk, he would have offered a few suggestions as to where the doc could cram it, sideways at that.

Then he realized the doc was talking again. "…connected to the suit via a transmitter at this end."   The doc pointed to the flat circular end. "Now, there is a lot of very interesting circuitry in that suit of yours, Nick, and this is the trigger, when exposed to water."

The doc reached down, picked up a beaker of water and slowly poured it over the molded piece of rubber in his hand. Instantly, flames shot through Nick's brain. Stimulation like he couldn't believe was traveling up and down his body; his cock felt like it was being tickled from the inside. Waves of erotic sensations ran up and down his body. His nipples seemed to have ripples of sensations hitting them over and over in a totally orgasmic sensation that whirled Nick's mind. His ass seemed to blast pure erotic sensations through his spine, and all these sensations earthed out in his brain and sent it twisting through a kaleidoscope of sensations.

Suddenly, it stopped, and starbursts stopped appearing in front of Nick's eyes. It was only when the sensations all stopped that Nick orgasmed. It was like being hit by a car after getting up from being hit by lightening. The sensation blew him away as, once again, sexual energy rocketed through him as he sent jets of sperm down the tube in his cock and the muscle spasms of orgasm ripped up his body through every nerve and engulfed him once again.

When it all stopped, Nick was amazed that he had any bones left in his body. He felt completely spent, like he had been turned inside out, dragged over fire and turned right-way out again. The doc was smiling. "Fun, wasn't it? And that was just one, there are ten in all. The best part is, you don't cum until the stimulation ends, and that can be a very long time if the trans-mitters keep in contact with water. Let me assure you, you won't know if you're in heaven or hell after about five minutes of that. But now, I must say goodbye, Mr. Douglas, as this is the last time I will see you."

Before his words could take root in Nick's still slightly spaced-out mind, the doc picked up a hood similar to the one

Nick had been wearing before, but this one came down further and seemed to be designed to be stretched over the top of the shoulders. When it was in place, Nick realized that the other major difference was that this one's visor was not clear. He was in darkness, until suddenly he could see again, but it was as if he was looking up at some rubber figure lying on a table, also hooded with a blacked-out gasmask hood. Then Nick realized that he was actually looking down on himself from above as the doc's red head appeared beside the figure on the table, then turned its head up and grinned.

Again, Nick heard words come from speakers near his ears. "You see, Mr. Douglas, this visor inside is actually a video screen. The camera is currently on top of you, but can be moved. It is incredibly tiny, no smaller than a full stop." He fiddled with something, and Nick felt slightly nauseous as the view blurred with movement and stopped over the tanks on the far side of the room.

The doc's voice again sounded in his ears. "It appears that the product is finished, Mr. Douglas, and our end game is about to be revealed."

Nick tried to work out what he was looking at. It appeared to be a long length of rubber that was being pulled out of the tank. From this angle, it looked like half a cylinder being stood up on its semi-circular end. Then it was laid down on its curved side and he saw that the face that should have been flat had a weird indent in it. He realized that the indent was shaped like a body, like a person lying with their legs slightly spread and their arms away from their sides with their fingers splayed.

A very nasty suspicion began to form in his head. Nick had not been terribly religious, but he began to pray to all and every god, goddess and devil that he was wrong about this. He felt hands pick his body up and begin to move him, although his view did not change. This was very strange sensation indeed. Then the orderlies appeared below him, or rather below the camera, carrying his body. As they lowered it toward the body indent, Nick felt his back come to rest against something. It was very comfortable and fit him perfectly. No gaps were between the suit and the sides of the indent. His fingers were each separated and pressed down into their individual grooves; his legs spread apart slightly and rested in their grooves.

Nick's mind was once again clear, the orgasm now forgotten in the face of this very new and very disturbing development. The half cylinder was lifted at one end and someone stepped forward holding what looking like a long black cylinder in his arms. Then they pulled a long flat piece off of it and he realized it was actually a roll of some black substance, probably rubber. The figure stepped up to the cylinder with Nick resting in it and began to wrap the material all around it. Nick felt a pressure on his front pressing him back into the already form-fitting indent. The process took a while because of a number of tubes from Nick's cock and breathing-and-food tube, but soon all that remained was a black surface with a slightly raised, human-shaped bump.

Nick saw the doc squat down beside his cocoon and run his hand over him and felt the hand through the layers of rubber. Then the doc's voice filled his ears. "This is a piece of good look for you, Mr. Douglas. Form-fitting. Of course, it won't stay like that if your muscles degrade, so that's why the same electrodes delivering those terribly arousing sensations will also stimulate your muscles from time to time to keep you in this precise shape. You know all about the various tubes and their purposes. And now, to complete this amusing little structure."

Nick watched as his half cylinder was stood up again on its flat ends. He felt the sensation of movement. He truly could not imagine what these sick bastards were doing. His mind had again gone numb. Thoughts like 'this can't be real;

soon I will wake up and be in my bed and none of this will have happened' were rushing through his head, bumping up against other pathetic lies, but below that was the dark voice at the back of his mind going, 'It's real. There is no escape.'

Michael positioned the upright half-cylinder into the fiberglass casing. Then the other half of the casing was moved against it to form the complete cylinder, open at the top. Nick's rubber prison was nearly complete. Michael manipulated the controls of the camera so it was looking directly down as a large pipe was hauled over. A person was standing on a ladder beside the cylinder, using strips of fiberglass and plaster to seal the two halves together. The end of the large pipe was rested in the empty half of the cylinder and the breathing, food, and piss tubes were held up above the opening by an orderly on another ladder.

Michael walked over to a pump and flicked a switch. Immediately, liquid rubber started to flow thought the thick hose into the empty space in the cylinder. Michael activated the microphone. "Liquid glass, Mr. Douglas. It will dry and solidify and then your entrapment will be complete. The majority of this is over. I will explain the rest when you're all dry and firm."

Michael stood and watched as the rubber slowly filled the cylinder, then went to attend to his own needs. This had been one hot scene, and it wasn't quite over. He wondered how Nick felt, feeling the warmth creep up from the tips of his toes to above his head. He wondered which would feel worse -- the warmth slowly creeping up or the warmth slowly cooling. Maybe he would do something like this to his slave and then pull him out and ask him.

Michael walked up to the cylinder. He almost didn't recognize it anymore. The outside had been painted and more plaster applied to reach the required texture. The ten rubber transmitters had been glued to the bottom, the fake leaves and branches added to the top. He knew Nick would be watching all this from the camera. He turned and faced where he knew the camera was.

"That's right, Mr. Douglas. You're a tree. In fact, this particular tree is going to be placed in a memorial garden out the back of the building you were trying so hard to stop Mr. Collins from constructing. There is even going to be a plaque dedicating the tree to your memory. There will be 'root' transmitters placed just below the ground and the tree will be watered regularly. Food and waste tanks will be hidden in the foliage and changed at night. Impressive, isn't it? It was a pleasure having you here, Mr. Douglas. I may stop by the garden one day with a watering can, I don't know. I am so busy, you know."

With that he smiled and walked out, leaving the artists to finish their work on the tree.

THREE MONTHS LATER

Susan walked down the path of the garden. She stopped and examined a pleasant-smelling lavender bush. She sighed; Nick wouldn't have been happy that the building had been built after he had worked so hard while alive to prevent it, but she felt he would have appreciated the garden. She and other members of the protest group had been surprised when Mr. Collins had erected the garden in Nick's memory, but he had said at his dedication speech that he had admired Nick's dedication and strong morals.

As she rounded a corner in the path and came to the center of the garden where the mighty oak dedicated to Nick had been planted, she was surprised to see Mr. Collins standing before the tree.

He turned as he heard her footsteps and smiled, nodding when he saw the wreath she carried. "Hello, young lady. Did you know Mr. Douglas?"

Susan smiled. Her feelings toward Tony Collins had changed since his dedication of the tree. "Yes, I was his girlfriend before…"

She felt tears well in her eyes. Then Mr. Collins was by her side, patting her shoulder. He took the wreath and gently laid it at the base of the tree. "Don't worry, young lady. I am sure that he is watching over us, wherever he is. Perhaps you would like to join me for coffee?"

Susan nodded. She and Mr. Collins stood at the tree, looking down at the plaque for a few more minutes, Mr. Collins still patting her gently on the shoulder. If Susan or anyone else looked very closely at the plaque, they might have noticed a small dot near the top, like a small glass lens. Mr. Collins gently took Susan by the hand and led her back down the path. As they reached the entrance, Mr. Collins turned to a small control panel. "Just one moment, young lady. I just need to put the sprinkler system on for an hour or so to keep things fresh."

The young man awoke inside a cage. He was naked. He struggled onto his hands and knees and looked around. He heard a voice to the right of him and he spun around to see where it was coming from. "Hello, Jason. My name is Dr. Michael. You've made a very powerful enemy. Does the name Tony Collins ring any bells?"

NO GOOD DEED GOES UNPUNISHED

An alarm buzzed. I stirred slightly in my sleep. I grumbled in general protest about the stupid beeping waking me up. I reached out with a hand and whacked around the area the noise was coming from until I made contact with the off button and rolled over and hugged my pillow, trying to get back to sleep. It was about then that I remembered I didn't even have an alarm clock.

Sitting up, I looked around. I didn't recognize the room I was in. I couldn't even remember how I got here, which is a first for me. I don't drink, so I have never had the misfortune of waking up and finding myself lying next to the long-lost ugly twin of Quasimodo. The bed was large and comfy and the sheets very soft. I was definitely alone, and the room had a slight 'hotel' look about it. Unless I had been left to cover the bill, I couldn't see any nasty surprises on the horizon. Something tight was around my groin area, and I reached down in annoyance. I don't wear undies or tight pants, so I wasn't sure why I would be feeling constricted in that area. It wasn't until I touched cold metal that I suddenly had the same sensation in my stomach that I imagine an explorer in the Amazon would get when he finds the local tribe's word for stranger is the same as their word for lunch.

I threw the sheets off me and stared in horror at my crotch. I was locked in a chastity belt. I jumped up and ran over to a closet door, which had a mirror on it. I turned and studied this new addition to my wardrobe with mounting panic. A heavy metal shield covered the front. With a bit of groping around, I was able to find that my balls were exposed and my cock was in some sort of tube that ran back between my legs. There was a small plate over my ass area. I found a raised area and managed to flip the plate open with my fingernail. At least I wouldn't explode from a massive build-up of shit unable to escape. The whole thing was held in place by a steel belt that ran around my waist above my hips, just tight enough that I couldn't slide it down.

I examined the lock; it was a combination one -- five tumblers in all. I quickly tried the usual numbers -- 11111, 00000, 12345. Unfortunately, whoever had set the combination had an IQ higher than 2.

I sat on the edge of the bed and tried to piece together my oddly-fractured memory of last night. I had finished work at a restaurant and had started walking home. I had been walking behind this guy who had suddenly tripped on an uneven piece of pavement and gone down hard. I stopped to help him up. He looked up, and I had caught a glimpse of a cheeky grin, blue eyes and a handsome face. "Thanks." He had a sexy voice, too. Then, suddenly, he had pointed a spray bottle at my face and squirted something at me. I had gasped as something cold and wet hit me in the face. I felt a slight burning sensation in my throat and nose, and then the world went dark.

I ground my teeth together. What a jerk. That's it -- next time I see someone trip, even if it's a little old nun, I am gonna kick them to make sure they don't get up in a hurry -- and run. I stood and walked over to the closet and opened it; there were clothes inside -- not my clothes, but they looked like the style of stuff I wear. I was a little creeped out by this, more than the belt really. It suggested that this had all been planned specifically for me. I scolded myself for being paranoid, and pulled on the clothes. On the next shelf I found a pair of shoes and socks, my size. This was not helping me relax. As weird as it sounds, I felt oddly violated, knowing that someone knew my measurements without my consent.

I laced up the shoes, walked over and opened the door to see what other surprises this day had in store for me. I walked out of the room and into a bigger room. Because I was sans wallet, I was slightly relieved to not find myself in a hotel foyer. There were two doors aside from the one I had come through, and right in the middle of the room was a small table with a note on it. I approached cautiously. I had barely been awake for more than half an hour, and I'd already had enough surprises to last me a lifetime.

I picked up the note and read it.

Hello Alex, (So much for thinking I was paranoid)

You're probably a little worried at the moment, but I assure you that you're in no danger. (Well, I felt better already.) *You have come to a crossroad. I would like to invite you on a little game. As you progress, you will receive numbers that correspond to the combination of the lock on your belt. If you choose not to play, please walk over to the blue door. The combination to the lock will be mailed to you in three months.* (Three damn months locked in this?!? Wait, they know where I live?!?!) *However, if you do choose to play, I can assure you that by the end of the day, you will have the combination to the lock on your belt. The other door is the beginning of this choice.*

I put the letter down. It seemed awfully rude of mysterious kidnappers not to sign letters.

I glanced back and forth at both doors. I had a slight uneasy feeling in my stomach. I *should* just run out the blue door and find my way to the nearest locksmith. But then again, this was a little more embarrassing than locking myself out of my car, and they knew where I lived, so how did I know I wouldn't just wake up again with another belt on? And if I played the game, I could have it off, and if the game got too kinky for my liking, then I could just stop and go to Plan B.

I stood drumming my fingers on the table top for a while. I finally sighed and walked over to the other door. It was black and had a picture of a small white rabbit on it. As reassuring as it is to walk through a door with the universal symbol of 'prey' on it, I still felt like maybe I had made the wrong choice.

The next room contained another small table with a box on it and another note. I picked it up and read it with the same feeling in my gut as a man reading his execution warrant.

> *Well, Alex, I am glad you decided to play. First off, a few rules.* (Oh, yay.) *Firstly, if you complete all challenges, you will receive the combination to the lock.* (I could live with that.) *The rest of the rules will be explained to you once you begin. Please use the items in the box. Please note -- the penalties for breaking the rules are rather harsh.*

I put the letter down and opened the box. Inside was a bottle of lube and a metal butt plug. There was also a phone and a set of car keys. There was a note stuck to the phone. It read:

> *This phone will only receive text messages. You cannot call out or send text messages yourself.*

I placed the phone down. There was also a set of car keys in the bottom of the box.

I decided to take care of the first small matter of business. I lubed up the plug and pried the small cover over my ass open and applied more lube to my asshole. I then slowly slid the plug up into my ass until I felt my sphincter clench shut around the thin base. I closed the cover and gave a small yelp as I felt the plug move weirdly inside me like it had been tugged. I tried to pry open the cover again, but it was stuck and wouldn't move. I had almost broken my nail twice when the phone suddenly beeped. I picked it up and read the first of many text message's for the day.

The plug you just inserted is actually a battery for the belt. The ass cover is now magnetically sealed. You were cleaned out last night, so you will not need to shit.

How very thoughtful. I swore rather badly, then wondered why a chastity belt would need a battery. I suddenly felt even less comfortable about this thing being in me, and tried to push out of my mind an image of where the key would go if it was powered by clockwork. I grabbed the car keys and phone, walked over to the door on the other side of the room, opened it and stepped out into the daylight.

I saw a jeep parked nearby. It was the only car around. In fact, there was really nothing else around. I was in the industrial area, and it was a Saturday. Silence echoed everywhere. I looked at the building I had just exited. It was just like all the other buildings in the area -- a box with a door and a few windows. I sighed and walked over to the jeep, opened the door and hopped in.

I could definitely handle cruising around in this all day. The seats were covered in black leather and there was even a GPS navigation system on the dashboard. I saw another note on the seat and read it.

Rule #1. Once you start, you may not back out. (So much for Plan B.) You will be sent GPS co-ordinates and must follow the directions given by the system. The car has satellite tracking. If you deviate from the path set, the police will be called and the car reported stolen. They will then be able to track the car. If you do not drive off within ten minutes of getting in the car, the police will be called and the car reported stolen. The first number to the combination lock is 1. The first GPS coordinates are…

I quickly started the car to power up the GPS system. I must have been in the car for about four minutes already. The system was thankfully easy to use. It entered the digits and gave me three lines of directions to follow. I put the car in gear and drove off.

It only took me about fifteen minutes to reach the destination. It was in another industrial warehouse-style area. I had only just pulled up when the phone suddenly beeped, indicating I had a message

Go inside building 2, undress, and put on what you find in the black box. Then enter the door on the other side of the room. If the door is not opened within five minutes from now, the police will be called.

I quickly hopped out of the car and locked the door. They sure didn't muck around with threats. I walked over to building 2, opened the door and walked in. I was in another plain room with another table in the middle of it; on the table was a black box. I walked over and opened the box. There was a note and a large metal circle and two smaller ones; they had a break in them. I realized they were a metal collar and two metal bracelets.

I opened the note and read it.

Strip and put on the items in the box. Go into the next room and touch nothing but what you're supposed to. Feel free to look around.

I placed the note down and started to strip off my clothes. I wondered how I was supposed to know what I was supposed to touch. I picked up the metal collar and looked at it. It was only about an inch and a half wide. I could see no way of opening it once it was on. The same went for the bracelets, but they were thicker. I sighed and put them on, hearing a heart-stopping click each time I closed them. It was not worth getting arrested for, that's for sure. I stepped through the door for the next room, and stopped in surprise.

In the middle of the room were three fuck benches, the sort where you kneel on one part while lying on another and your arms are on rests at your side. With your arms and wrists tied, your ass is at the perfect height for fucking, spanking or whatever. On two benches were two other lads; the third was empty. It was now obvious what I wasn't supposed to touch, but I had been told I could look. As I moved to look at one lad, I noticed that the door had shut behind me and there was no handle on this side of the door. No doubt I would have to get on the bench to see what happened next.

Neither of the two guys lifted their heads to look at me. They were naked except for the same metal collars and wrist bands as me. Their ankles were strapped in, but that was it. Their hands were palm up and they were gripping handles that were on the sides of the armrests. I saw that their cocks were strapped into tubes, but couldn't see what they were for. Curiouser and curiouser.

Both guys were rock-hard. I squatted down in front of one

and he looked at me with pleading eyes. He had a large butterfly gag in his mouth. From the looks of his bulging cheeks, I could see that the tube was connected to the fuck bench. They also both had butt plugs up their asses with wires running into the fuck bench. The word 'battery' kept trying to nudge its way to the front of my thoughts, but I kept knocking it back. The guys could just get up, but they were probably told that if they moved, they would be shocked in the butt. I moved over to the last bench.

They were positioned so we faced each other in a sort of circle. The sooner I was in place, the sooner we could all get the fuck out of here. I knelt down on the pads for my legs and then I was kneeling, bent at the waist, so I was lying on the top. I placed my arms with my palms facing up on the armrests and gripped the handles. I laid my head on the edge of the bench and bit down on the gag. No sooner had my neck made contact with the edge of the bench than I felt a tug on my collar, and when I tried to move my head I found I couldn't. I let go of my handles and tried to lift my arms up to my neck, but found I couldn't lift my wrists off the armrests. I realized the damn things must be magnetized to the damn bench. No wonder the other guys couldn't move, either; and with their gags in, couldn't warn me about it. No sooner had I worked this out than I felt the gag in my mouth inflate and fill my mouth.

Suddenly a voice issued out over the speakers. It was smooth and deep, and sounded oddly familiar. "Well, now that we are all here, the game can begin. For those of you who have come late, Alex, I will fill you in. These two lads have been here for the past few hours being fed Gatorade. They have managed to provide a lot of piss, which is being stored below in a tank. This is a test of endurance. Your armrests will soon be released and you will be able to curl your arms up at the elbow. The armrests will then gradually return to their original position. With more pressure, whoever manages to keep their armrests up the longest will not be force-fed piss. Whoever's arms go down first will receive a shock in the ass, as well as piss. This includes you, Alex. Your belt has some interesting surprises. This will continue until all the piss is drained, and then you will be released in the reverse order you arrived at fifteen-minute intervals."

The voice stopped and I felt my armrest suddenly move. I curled my arms up and tensed my arms as tight as I could. I looked over. Neither of the other two seemed overly muscled, but that didn't mean they weren't packing some strength in their arms. I felt the handles being pulled down again and strained to keep my arms bent. I saw the other two doing the same. The handles were being slowly pulled back down. I closed my eyes, bit down hard on the gag, and pulled with as much might as I could. The problem was that the bracelets were starting to bite into my arms as well.

Soon my muscles were on fire and I had no choice but to let the armrests return to their position. Mine had barely touched when I heard a muffled noise. I opened my eyes. One dude was already bucking around in his restraints, trying to shake his head and squealing into his gag. Obviously, some serious volts were being pumped into his butt.

Suddenly, my mouth was full of the taste of piss and I felt my cheeks swelling. I had no choice but to swallow it down as fast as I could. The disgusting, sour aftertaste made me wanna spit, but I couldn't; as suddenly as it had started, it stopped and I felt my handles loosen again.

I curled my arms up, tensed them and waited. I felt the handles begin to tug again, and suddenly the strain, plus me tensing, caused my arm to cramp. I tried to yelp in pain and automatically tried to straighten my arm, pretty much slamming the armrest back down. Instantly my mouth filled with sour piss again and I felt like someone had pinched my ass hard as my butt plug suddenly pumped some electricity through me.

With my ass spasming with the shocks and me trying not to choke on the foul liquid in my mouth, I couldn't see what the others were doing. This continued for what seemed like ages. Six more times we were forced to hold onto the handles for as long as we could. I think one of the other dudes got a cramp like me at one time. I managed to get no piss once, came second four times and last again because my arm was still sore from the cramp.

Finally I felt the gag in my mouth deflate and the door clicked open. I found I could move my head. I hastily lifted my head and spat out the foul gag, then spat a few times on the floor to clear the taste of piss out of my mouth. I quickly moved toward the door, massaging my sore arms.

Back in the other room, it seemed there had been a visitor. My old clothes were gone and now there was a pair of heavy looking boots, a pair of leather jeans and a tight black t-shirt. I pulled the jeans on and noticed that there was a belt sewn onto the outside. The buckle of it was like a seatbelt, but without the handle. I would be able to do it up but not undo it. It seemed like I was just getting deeper and deeper into trouble.

I also had no way of taking off the damn collar around my neck or the bracelets on my arms. I clipped the belt shut with another feeling of impending doom and pulled on the T. I reached for the boots. They were large biker-style boots, with buckles instead of laces. I pulled them on, and as I was tightening the buckles, noticed they had nails in the soles of them. I had a happy little thought of driving the damn things so far up the ass of whoever was playing with me like this that they would be able to undo the buckles with their tongue.

The phone beeped. I reached over, grabbed it and read the message.

The second combination is 12. The GPS coordinates are on the seat of the car. If it is not moving within five minutes, the police will be called.

I was of half a mind to call their bluff and let them rock up here and then get the other two to help me explain what was going on. But I decided against it and raced back out to my mobile prison.

As I drove to the next destination, it dawned on me -- I was really in a pickle now. I was locked in pants and a collar with two metal bracelets on my wrists. I was in a car that could at any moment be reported as stolen if I didn't do as I was told. I had no I.D. or anything to prove who I was. I was locked in a chastity device that could shock my ass, and who the hell knows what else. My mouth tasted like sour piss and I was driving into even more trouble. If I tried to bail out, the cops would be called, and even if I managed to get out of that situation, I would have to then figure out not only how the hell to get myself out of these damn pants, but also how to get the collar off from around my neck and the bracelets off my wrists. And THEN I would've broken the rules, so who knows what these sick bastards behind all of this might do? Tip the cops off to where I lived, or worse? Let the damn thing up my ass shock me till it went flat. As I was thinking about all of this, I nearly missed a turn, and with my heart thudding in my chest, I thought about how close I had just come to being in deep shit. I concentrated on driving.

I again pulled up outside a reasonably plain-looking building. If ever I was to learn not to judge a book by its cover it was now. I walked inside and there was the familiar note on the table.

This task is a little easier. You simply have to

gather the four items in the next   room. Mind your step.

I walked into the next room and looked around. There were four small tables around the room, two near the walls and the other two near the center of the room. I remembered the end of the letter and looked down.

About two steps in front of me was a line formed by red tiles. After that there was a crazy, raised pattern on the floor. Here and there were some smooth black tiles. I supposed I might trip on the raised area if I wasn't careful, and maybe the black tiles were a little slippery. Somehow I thought it might get a little more complicated than that.

I walked forward, and as soon as I stepped over the red tiles, a TV that I hadn't noticed on the far wall turned on. The words *"Be back across the line before the timer runs out"* appeared on it. Then it was replaced by a countdown from four minutes. I very much doubted it would take me four minutes to gather all the gear and be back across the line, but I hurried forward nonetheless.

I had just carefully stepped over a raised area on the floor when suddenly, a jolt of pain ran through my nuts. I yelped and doubled over. The pain continued, and I clenched my legs together in desperation before it stopped. I looked up, and the words *"Mind your step"* were on the TV. They were replaced soon by the countdown.

I looked back down. The raised areas were not just a random pattern; they formed a maze.

I glanced up at the clock; I had about three minutes left. I looked for the nearest table and tried to figure out a way to it without stepping over a raised line. I shuffled carefully between the lines until I was able to reach the table. With a little experimentation, I was able to find I could reach across the raised lines as long as no part of the belt went over it.

I reached and grabbed the item on the table -- it was a large gag. I looked up at the clock; I had a minute and thirty seconds left. I hurriedly strolled back to the red tiles and managed to get across them with twenty seconds on the clock.

The TV turned off and I examined the gag. There was nothing unusual about it. I placed it on the floor, careful not to let the bit touch the floor, since I had a fair idea as to whose mouth it would be going in. I stood back up and tried to work out a way to the next table before I stepped across the red tiles. Once I had it in my mind, I stepped over the tiles.

This time the words *"Black will set you back. Watch your step"* flashed up on the screen before the countdown began. This must mean that if I stepped on a black-tiled area, I would get a shock as well. My route I had chosen didn't require me this, though, so I hurried forward. I managed to get the second and third items -- a leather jacket and a leather hood (this was looking bad) without any trouble. But when I stepped back across the red tiles a fifth time, the words *"Penalty points"* appeared before the usual warning about black and watching my step.

This time I only had three minutes. I had left the most distant table for last and was now wishing I had gone for it first. I moved as quickly as I could, but each time only made it about three-quarters of the way before I had to turn around and head back before running out of time. I didn't lose any more time the sixth and seventh time I stepped across, but I wasn't getting any closer.

There were a few black tiles in the road. I decided I was going to have to tolerate a shock and get this over with. I made it to a black tile and stepped over it, gritting my teeth and bracing for the shock. It never came. I opened my eyes in surprise. Apparently, "the black will set you back" was a bunch of crap. This left a relatively clear path for me, so I strode forward toward the table and it wasn't until I actually stood on a black tile that I found a problem, namely that my foot was stuck there.

I tried lifting it, but it was stuck to the tile. Probably more magnets. I looked up. The clock continued to count down, and I still couldn't move my foot. I had no choice but to wait for the clock to reach zero, and suddenly felt both my balls and my ass tingle in a big way. My foot was released and I stumbled back toward the tiles, basically having to crawl over them because I was in so much pain.

I lay on my back, gasping for a little while, then stood up and tried again. I made it to the table and was careful to step over the black tiles and to stay within the raised area. I crossed the finish line with the last item, a pair of fist mitts. I wearily bent over and gathered everything up as the door clicked open for me.

I was really feeling the plug in my butt now because of all the moving around I had done in the room. I noticed a new note on the table, picked it up and read it.

Place jacket on, get in passenger side of car, and get some rest. Next combination is 9.

I placed the jacket on and zipped it up. The weather outside was sunny and warm, so I was glad no one was around to see me make a fool of myself. I walked outside and felt the sun beating down on my now leather-clad body. I bristled at the indignity of being forced to wear this crap in such weather. I unlocked the passenger side and threw the keys on the driver's seat and buckled on the gag tight. I had no desire to get a shock to my ass or balls for not following orders. The inside of the car was already hotter than outside, and I left the door open as I pulled the hood on.

It had a zipper and laces at the back. It had two small holes at the nose to breathe through, but that was it. I managed to pull the mitts on my hands and laid them in my lap. I had no way of doing them up. I was sitting there in darkness, heating up real fast. I was just about to rip off the mitts and pull the damn hood off when a pair of hands grabbed me.

I nearly jumped out of the seat in shock. Then, a strong hand pushed my head back and suddenly I felt my collar tug against my neck. I realized I couldn't pull my head forward. This was getting annoying. I tried to raise my feet but found they wouldn't leave the floor of the jeep. It was a damned bondage box on wheels!!! I felt the guy tighten the mitts and clip them together. Then I felt him pull something on the hood. I realized it must be a ball cap to conceal the fact that I was wearing a leather mask. There was a click and a faint hiss. I realized it was a tape recorder.

Suddenly, the same voice from the other room issued near my ear. "And so, Alex, we have come to the end of the part where you have to drive yourself around. Your next destination will be revealed in good time. Just sit back, relax, and enjoy the ride." I heard the player being clicked off and I heard my door slam. A few seconds later, the driver's side opened and suddenly we were off.

We didn't have to drive for long before we came to a stop again; there was a steep decline before we stopped so I am guessing we were in an underground parking lot. I heard the driver's side door open and close and heard my door open. I felt hands loosen the straps on my fist mitts. I waited a while, but nothing more happened.

I suddenly could move my head again. I shook the mitts off my hands and managed to get the hood and gag off in short order. I looked around. We were indeed in a carpark. It was empty except for the jeep. There was no one else in the area, either. There was a door on the far side of the parking area, and I hopped out and headed for it. I didn't have the phone anymore and the dude had taken the keys with him. As I approached, I noticed there was a sign above the door. It read:

CLUB WONDERLAND

Well, that sounded chirpy.

I looked around. Whoever had designed this place had done so with the intent of building the physical definition of the word 'irony'. The decorations of the empty club put the G in gothic, possibly the O, T, H, I and C as well. I tried not to make contact with any furniture as I walked along, mainly because most of it was spiked. There was a familiar small table not far ahead; I wondered if it was the same one.

I picked up the note that was beside a small bottle.

Well, Alex. The end is almost in sight. In anticipation of your following the rules, the next combination is 3.

I put down the note and picked up the bottle. There was a small note attached to it. It said *Drink me.*

My first thought was "Like hell!" However, I didn't seem to be in much of a position to argue. There was very little that could be locked onto me that hadn't already been done. I turned the bottle over, in the vague notion of checking for a skull and cross bones. Ya know, if you drink something labeled thusly it is almost certain to disagree with you sooner or later.

When no such markings were obvious, I sighed and pulled the cork out of the top. I realized that it didn't hiss or bubble when I did, so I tilted my head back and tipped the entire bottle down my throat. It tasted pleasantly of cherry-tart; I was surprised.

I put the bottle down and waited. Nothing happened. I relaxed. Someone was obviously just messing with me.

That's when I felt like I was hit by a giant marshmallow hammer. As I fell towards the floor, I noticed that even the carpet had a spider's web pattern on it.

I groaned as I opened my eyes. I felt cool air hit my body, which meant I was naked, which was nice. I fully opened my eyes and realized the inability to move wasn't due to the after-effects of whatever I had drunk. It was because I was held down with leather straps that were spaced about every four inches up the entire length of my body. I was still in the chastity belt. I could see all of this because I was looking up at a mirror of myself. I then noticed that I was in a coffin, which caused me to make some very loud noises into my gag and struggle rather earnestly against my bonds until someone appeared overhead.

"Hello, Alex."

I looked up at him. He looked very familiar. He was smiling slightly. He was older than me, perhaps in his late thirties. He had a neat haircut and a trimmed goatee, a very neat suit and two very wicked blue eyes.

He continued grinning as he spoke to me. "You don't remember me, do you? Well, let me help. About two weeks ago, you stopped a gentleman who had dropped his wallet, and you handed it back to him."

My eyes widened. That's where I had seen him before. I had been walking behind him and he had pulled a pocket watch out of his trouser pocket and glanced at it and at the same time his wallet had fallen out. I had grabbed it, stopped him and handed it back to him. He had been very grateful for such an 'excellent display of honesty' and had tried to give me a reward. I had been in a hurry and it was really no big deal, so I had thanked him, but said 'no' and hurried off.

I realized he was speaking again and concentrated on what he was saying. "Well, Alex, you modestly refused a reward for returning my wallet, so I felt I would try and surprise you. I followed you home and then had a private detective tail you and dig up some information on you so I could put together a suitable reward. Never let it be said that Richard Carroll leaves a good deed unrewarded. I was very pleasantly surprised to find out about your darker side, because it seems we share a passion for similar things, although I, personally, am a top. I am over here briefly from the States on business, so I thought I would, ah, invite you to come home and have a few play sessions with me. This, I am afraid, is the reason for the coffin. I will be flying back on my personal jet but didn't have time to procure you a fake passport and documents. Human remains are never inspected by customs, so we will pass you off as a cadaver. I assure you, however, that I intend to keep you alive and very well. And now, before we settle you down for your long flight, I am, as ever, a man of my word. The last combination for your lock is 5. As I promised, you would have the combination to your lock by the end of the day, and so you do."

He then knelt and picked up a small syringe that was on the floor. I watched wide-eyed with terror as he pressed it against the arm I was straining to pull free. I felt a mild sting and then felt calming waves of darkness sweep over me.

The gentleman walked through the corridor of his office. He smiled at men and women as he passed, and they smiled back. On the drive home, he hummed a little tune to himself. He drove an old Chrysler with tailfins. His garage also housed BMWs and other expensive cars, but old cars held a certain charm that could not be ignored. They spoke of a time when it wasn't speed and gadgets that mattered, but reliability, and building something that would last a lifetime.

He pulled up to the gatehouse and nodded to the guard on duty, who returned the nod and waved him through. He continued to drive into a nice neighborhood; large sprawling houses lined the road on either side. Massive oaks were also present along the streets. All power and phone lines and other such eyesores were buried underground and carefully out of reach of the mighty trees' ever-curious roots. He pulled into a driveway in front of a very impressive house. He waved to the neighbor pruning her rosebush by her steps. She smiled a lovely smile; no doubt it had cost her husband a lot of money, but the effect made for a pleasant look.

He whistled a little tune as he strode into his house. He loosened the tie around his neck, walked into a library and over to a shelf that looked just like all the others around it -- until he pushed it and it swung inward. He strolled through the previously-concealed door and into another world.

Richard approached the table. On it lay a bound figure. A leather strait jacket encased the upper torso in an inescapable hug. The victim had a spreader bar at the knees and another at the ankles. He was in rubber shorts with his penis and balls exposed. His cock was cathetered and the tube ran to a bag taped on his leg. The ankle restraints that connected to the ankle spreader bar also had chains connecting them to the sides of the table, which had slightly raised edges; in short, the lad was going nowhere. From the nose up, his face was free; from the nose down, there was a half-mask strapped over his face. A tube was running into the center of it and disappeared under the table. It was connected to a bottle filled with a very rich protein and vitamin mixture, as well as a few other chemical cocktails to produce something that was basically a complete liquid diet. Richard knew the taste was not fantastic.

As soon as the figure on the table caught sight of Richard, he began to moan and grunt very loudly through his gag. It was clear that he was not asking for directions to the bus stop. He also started to struggle. It was an impressive sight. He bucked his hips and did half sit-ups before collapsing back with a frustrated grunt. He tried desperately to close his legs.

Richard watched this with an amused look on his face for a little while, then walked over and firmly pushed the lad down on the table. The boy looked up and there was no mistaking the fear in his eyes.

Richard smoothed the boy's now sweat-soaked hair off his forehead as he spoke. "Well, Peter, it looks like you're still full of beans. Ready for your milking?"

The boy began to grunt and whine through the gag and shook his head fiercely from side to side.

Richard raised an eyebrow and frowned in confusion. "No? But Peter, we chatted about this, remember? I asked you online what you wanted and you said to be fed a cup of cum. Now, I do remember I made it very clear that I do not participate in unsafe sex, my dear boy. So that means you will have to supply that, and I am a man of my word, Peter. I promised you a scene of your choice, and so I will provide one. Now, let's see how you're doing here."

With those words, he walked over to a small bar fridge on

the wall. He pulled out a glass jar about the size of a large, cylinder-shaped glass and swirled the contents. Thick and viscose, the contents were impossible to mistake for anything other than semen. Richard knew it was mixed well with a preserving agent to keep it from congealing and going off. He spoke as he swirled the contents of the glass in front of the boy's eyes. The boy did not move; his eyes never left the container in Richard's hand.

"Well, this isn't bad for three days' effort. Another day or two and you should have enough for a cup, then a quick swig, and my obligation to you shall be fulfilled. Well, no point in wasting time."

He bent down and connected the valve at the top of the jar to an output on a machine resting under the table. This seemed to snap the boy out of his trance, because he once again began to whine into the gag and buck around on the table. Richard ignored his muffled pleas as he slipped the catheter out of the boy's penis and discarded it. He made a very great show of lubing the inside of a cylinder attached to a tube that led to the machine. He activated the machine and a soft sucking noise filled the room. He lowered the device onto the boy's flaccid penis, allowing the tube to suck the cock in, then pulled it off until this motion caused the penis to grow. The boy groaned with misery and lust as Richard finally slid the entire cylinder onto the boy's cock.

While the boy continued to moan as the devious machine did its job, Richard walked back to the fridge and pulled out a syringe in the fridge. The syringe was fat and filled with liquid. It did not have a needle on the end. Peter's eyes followed his movement as he walked back over to the table. Peter was obviously unable to do anything about what would happen next. Richard removed the tube from the boy's gag and inserted the end of the syringe into the hole, and slowly pushed the plunger down. Peter had no choice but to swallow. The liquid contained

Sildenafil, which was an active ingredient in Viagra. The dosage was sufficient to ensure that the boy's cock stayed hard for at least the next eight or nine hours.

Richard then walked over to the door leading to another area of his hidden dungeon. When he did eventually free Peter and send him on his way, he knew the boy would be a lot more careful in the future about what he asked for.

When Richard entered my room, he was wearing leather jeans and a tight leather shirt. He had a good body and obviously worked hard to keep it like that. I wasn't going anywhere. I was strapped into a bondage chair. I am not sure exactly how long I had been out, or even how long it had been since I awakened like this.

I had peed once. There was a bucket resting below my penis, obviously for this purpose. I tried to shift in the chair but that was impossible. A fat strap ran around my forehead, pulling my head firmly back into the padded headrest. My elbows were strapped and my hands rested on a board that covered my lap. My fingers were spread and each one was strapped down to the board; my wrists were also strapped down. There was a thick strap around my waist and more holding me at the knees and ankles. As far as I could tell, I didn't have the chastity device on anymore, which was a relief. But I suspected that far worse things lay on the horizon for me. I was right about that...

Richard apologized very politely for not being there when I woke up. I would have been less polite if I had been able to talk, but I had a gag firmly strapped in place. The bit filled my mouth and stopped me from making any coherent noise. He then strapped a collar around my neck that had a weird box on the side. I felt something poking me in the neck. He told me it was a shock collar, similar to the ones used to train unruly dogs. I got the point fairly quickly.

He first cuffed my hands together before unstrapping me. He even removed the gag. I remained silent, not trusting myself to not say something that would undoubtedly get me zapped. 'You sick bastard' would have been one of the nicer phrases. I considered very briefly trying to make a run for it. But he held the remote up, and I stood absolutely still.

Richard smiled. "Well, now, let's get you dressed for some fun, Alex."

I had no idea of how much time had passed. I had more important things to worry about. I had a Catch-22 situation.

Richard told me this was the 22 room. When he said that, I assumed that it was simply a reference number. I bit down hard on my gag to stifle a moan of frustration and discomfort.

I looked around at my fellow lesson-learners. Across from me was a guy suspended; he was bound tightly in a leather sleep sack. His head poked out the end in a gas mask with a large, clear face visor. He had a posture collar on, so his head was kept straight; at about face level was suspended a large bag. A tube ran from the bag to his mouth. I wasn't sure what was in the bag, but no matter -- it was a fair amount of liquid.

The guy's cock and balls were hanging out of the sack. He had a rubber sheath over his cock, the tube of which ran down and ended in another bag. This one was resting on the floor on what appeared to be a set of scales, except the weight seemed to be counting down; the display was a large digital screen showing bright, glowing red numbers. Every now and again it would drop slightly, obviously when he peed.

There were wires running from the scales to his balls. Each time the number on the scale dropped down, he would start to writhe and struggle and I could hear muffled screams. Each time he struggled, he would swing wildly from side to side for longer and longer intervals. I guessed that the scales were also delivering electric shocks to him, and in increasing amounts as he filled the bag with more piss. I wondered what would happen when he got it down to zero; he probably did, too. The upside, and the true 69 catch in it -- his balls had a chain hanging from them. There were something like six or seven huge padlocks on the chain. The end was connected to an odd pulley system. Basically, as he drank more from the bag of liquid, it rose higher and also took up more of the slack on the chain; this was relieving the strain on his balls. Basically, he was torturing himself as well as removing part of his torment.

A tug on my nuts quickly brought me back to my own situation. Richard had first handed me a rubber one-piece; entry was via the back. While he stood with the remote held causally by him, I had pulled and tugged the suit on. The ends of the hands ended in mitts, so, using my flipper-like hands, I pulled the zipper of the suit up. Richard then stepped forward with a heavy leather straitjacket held in front of him. I obediently slipped my arms into the sleeves and stood still while he wrapped my arms around me in a hug. I felt him tugging on straps at the back. I also heard a number of clicks which I assumed were padlocks. My heart rate increased slightly each time I heard a click.

He then pulled the straps under my crotch and fastened those as well. He stood and I felt him fiddling with the zipper of the rubber suit. I heard a click and then he ran a chain around my neck, threaded it through a D-ring on the front of the straitjacket and locked the two ends together with a padlock. He then told me he had locked the zipper to the chain so I couldn't get either the straitjacket or rubber suit off without first getting the padlock at the front of my neck unlocked. With my arms trapped in the straitjacket sleeves, this would be a bit of a problem.

He then took a small key on a key ring and threaded it through the links of the chain next to the lock. "There you go, Alex. That's the key to all the locks holding you in those suits, so you can get out when you get tired of the scene." It took all my effort not to kick him.

Richard then pushed me back to the bondage seat and I sat down. He reached around the side of the chair and pulled out a pair of twenty-hole rangers, very nice! I eagerly slipped each foot into the boot he held up and watched while he laced up the black leather boots. The white laces looked awesome against the black of the rubber and the boot leather. When each was laced tightly, he stood up. There was now a massive bulge in the front of my rubber suit. He smiled when he saw it and then told me to open wide. I sighed and opened my mouth, knowing what was coming next. Sure enough, he pushed a large gag into my mouth. The gag filled my mouth and pushed my tongue firmly down, making any coherent words impossible. Richard then unbuckled the collar, helped me up, and led me to this room.

Once inside, Richard took me over to a raised area. It was a plank with a semi-circle cut out in the center of it. It was resting on a piece of stainless steel, which had vapor rising from it. Because I couldn't feel any heat, I assumed it was cold. My suspicions were confirmed when Richard helped me squat down and I saw that the plank was on a block of ice.

Richard had no problems getting me to step up onto the platform; he merely poked me with the remote -- a gentle reminder that he could use the remote for other reasons. I quickly obeyed. I stood still and I heard him behind me fiddling with something.

I wasn't really paying that much attention to what he was doing because I was too busy looking at the room's other member. He was naked except for heavy leather restraints around his wrists and ankles and a thick gag. The ankle and wrist restraints were kept on by some very big, shiny padlocks. He was standing between two poles. The set-up was like those machines you see in the gym, where the guy stands there and pulls down on a handle attached to wire from the top of the pole, lifting weights as he pulls the handle downward across his body.

This guy definitely looked like he would know how to handle one of these. 'General beefiness' would be the phrase I would use to describe him. He was staring daggers at Richard, I assume, because Richard was behind me; he was glaring in my general direction and I don't recall offending anyone with a build like that. I think I would have made a point of NOT offending anyone built like that.

His 69 position was devious, yet simplistic. As long as he kept the handles down low, they would not tug on his nuts, which had a parachute harness around them and was attached to the handles by rope. His wrist restraints were locked to the handles and as far as I could tell, the handles would only go down as far as his belly button, meaning he was unable to free his nuts of the harness. Now, the tricky bit -- pulling the handles down meant lifting the weights, and they were certainly some big ones. Even with his arms locked as they seemed to be, he was straining to keep the handles down. Even as I watched I saw them inch up slightly.

I was disturbed from my perving on the muscled hunk by the presence of something cold against my ass. I yelped into my gag and tried to shift slightly. I had not even noticed that he had unzipped the rubber suit over the ass area. I didn't get a chance to get away from the intruder. A quick push from Richard, some blinding white stars in front of my eyes, and a scream muffled by the gag in my mouth and the cold metal object was in my ass. It kept going in, and I kept struggling, eventually standing on tiptoes to try to escape it. That's when Richard stopped.

I tried to turn and see what the hell was going on, because he definitely now had my attention. I could sort of see what was going on -- he had some sort of dildo on a stick arrangement; apparently, he could raise and lower the pole accordingly. He was now tightening the nut that held it in place and ignoring my muffled grunts. He then stood up and moved to the front. He unzipped the front part of the suit and pulled my nuts out, snapped a parachute harness around my nuts and stretched it right down. I was torn between lowering my feet to take the strain off my nuts, and staying as I was, so that no more of the huge dildo ended up inside me.

My ass informed me that the thing got wider the further down you went. In fact, it was making a lot of noise about that particular fact. I bit down on the gag and managed to ignore the pain in my balls. Finally, Richard stood up again and I looked down. My nuts were tied off to somewhere under the board upon which I was standing.

I realized Richard was speaking and focused on what he was saying. "…you now and go tend to some other matters. I will be switching off the cooler plate beneath you, so the ice will melt. Incidentally, your nuts are tied off to an O-ring frozen in the ice. Have fun now."

My situation was rather straightforward. The ice melted, I grew tired of standing on tiptoes and I slowly sank onto the giant object violating my ass. However, as the ice melted, the ring attached to my balls got looser and looser. Apparently, the string connecting it to the harness was slightly elastic, because I could feel the ring being tugged. I again made an annoyed noise into my gag and felt the dildo slide a little further into my protesting asshole.

It was probably a good thing that I wouldn't be sending

any postcards home about this particular holiday. While they would make for an interesting read, I very much doubt that my friends and family would find them all that amusing.

Richard was humming along to light Calvary playing on the radio in the kitchen when the noise of happy suburbia was shattered by the sounds of a powerful engine. He glanced out a window and sighed as a massive humvee roared up his driveway and stopped inches from the bumper of his Chrysler. With a mixture of amusement and annoyance, he watched as the driver's side door swung open and a young man basically exploded from the vehicle. His nephew, Brett, never seemed to move at a pace slower then full steam ahead.

Two other figures emerged from the vehicle, but Richard paid them little heed. Brett was always flanked by a pair of muscle-bound brutes wherever he went -- not that he was a small figure himself; his biceps rippled under the tight sleeves of his shirt like oiled snakes in a sack.

Richard arrived at the door just in time to hear a random and erratic series of knocks beat against it. He winced, visualizing scratches on the three-hundred-year-old, hand-carved imported wood. One of these days he would take that boy over his knee.

He opened the door and his nephew flew into the house. "Hey, unc! How are you? Still a dirty old fart? Good, good. Now I need to borrow some items from your bitch pen for some fun this weekend." The whole lot poured in like bullets from a machine gun.

Richard could not help but smile. His nephew had a cute, innocent face, and a soul so black that coal sparkled in comparison. The fact that his sexual tastes were nearly identical to Richard's made him very fond of the lad. He paid no heed as

Twiddle Dee and Twiddle Dum lumbered in through the door.

He waved a hand toward the library. "Certainly, my boy, but please don't make a mess, and then kindly remove that monstrosity from my driveway!"

He turned and chuckled to himself as the lad zipped into the library. He had played a large part in his nephew's upbringing and emotional support when it became apparent he would not be fathering any brats, nor marrying some ice queen country club wench. Brett's useless parents had been less than supportive to what they saw as a possible scandal. Richard turned as he heard Brett emerge from the library. He waved the lad off and watched through the window as the two lumbering oafs dumped a pair of leather hockey bags in the back of the hummer. He winced in sympathy for the two boys in those bags. He returned to his task of preparing some dinner and smiled as he thought of the things he had in store for Alex.

I had been struggling against my bonds, impaled on the damned dildo, my balls finally free of abuse when, out of nowhere, some dude (admittedly, a very hot dude) had appeared and looked at me. I imagine I would have had an expression on my face similar to that of a deer caught in the headlights.

He looked me up and down. "Okay, guys, grab this one as well. Looks like some fun."

Before his words had truly sunk in, a meaty paw came around from behind me and a rag had been pressed over my mouth and nose. I gasped in shock. The darkness swirled in.

I groaned and opened my eyes slightly. Sunlight stabbed painfully into them, so I squeezed them shut again. I felt warm. I was naked and lying on sand. Considering some of the places I have found myself waking up in lately, this was not too bad.

I felt something heavy around my neck. I sighed to myself; no doubt, rinsing sand from unusual spots would be the least of my problems. I heard some groans to my left and right. Curiosity won out over my mind screaming 'ignorance is bliss!' I squinted open an eye and looked around -- lying next to me was another naked figure, heavy metal collar locked around his neck. I couldn't see much beyond him. I didn't want to roll over and make it apparent that I was awake, or, more accurately, make myself a moving target.

I wondered if this sudden change in circumstances was a good thing. I was still debating the wisdom of moving when a bucket load of icy cold water slammed into me. I gasped and my eyes flew open. I heard another gasp like mine and some groans. Knowing that the gig was up, I sat up and looked around.

The first thing I noticed was that there was a chain attached to my collar, preventing me from moving. It disappeared into the sand near my feet. I gave it a tug and found that it was not moving at all. I noticed five chains at regular intervals and five guys all sitting up and looking around. We all had similar builds and seemed to be about the same height, although this was a tad hard to be sure of, considering we were all lying in the sand.

Someone cleared his throat nearby, and five collared heads turned simultaneously toward the noise. There was the drop-dead handsome dude who had grabbed me from my impalement predicament. He was standing between two muscular dudes.

He flashed a 1000-watt smile. "Well, now, you may all be wondering why you're here today. Well, you're here to participate in a little game." My heart nearly stopped at those words. I was having major deja'vu, except I was naked on a beach attached to a chain buried in the ground with four other guys, instead of trapped in a chastity belt running around town. Despite this little difference, it was essentially the same.

I noticed that the dude was still talking, so I refocused on the words that would no doubt spell out my doom. "There can only be one winner, and each round will eliminate one person. I might point out at this stage that if you lose the round, there will be penalties. Now, behind you all is a shovel. Free yourselves and we will move on to the next part."

He walked over to an area were there was a chair set up under a sunshade. I noticed now that behind him there were guys moving, carrying gear around. I didn't bother trying to see why. I was more interested in the shovel behind me. It was one of those small, collapsible ones you take camping to dig a toilet hole. Now I was going to dig a hole to get myself out of shit.

I frantically shoveled away, trying not to get my shovel caught in the chain. The dude to my right tossed a shovel full of sand in my hole and I returned the favor with interest. Whether or not it was intentional, I didn't know, but he was a lot more careful to get his dirt to go behind him from then on. I wasn't paying attention to what was going on around me with the others. I was only aiming on trying to get to the bottom of the hole. Sand stuck to my body and sweat was stinging my eyes. Then my shovel finally hit something with a clunk. I grabbed my chain and heaved -- a little too hard. The box that had been buried at the bottom of the hole flew up and I fell backwards. I scrambled up and out of the hole and lay there panting. Digging a hole with a chain whacking against your naked, sand-covered body is not what I would call fun.

I looked around to see what the hell was going on around me. One other dude had finished. Looking at the empty hole, he had been the one who had flung a shovelful of soil into my hole. One look at his eyes before he turned his head away told me that there had been nothing unintentional about it. I would have to keep my eye on that one.

I looked back. One other dude was just climbing out of his hole now, covered in sand. Two guys were left going for it. The problem was, one had accidentally dug too close to the other dude's, and the wall between the two holes had collapsed into his hole. The other dude won, hands down.

We were left with a trench about a meter deep and about five meters long. The creator of this little hell stood up and walked over. I now saw there were were about six muscled guys hanging around now and that more vehicles were pulling up. The guys who were unloading things had moved a lot closer since we began digging, and definitely seemed to be getting some sort of party ready. I saw kegs and ice.

No one was paying us any attention. Our tormenter stretched lazily. I felt my cock twitch and reminded myself that this was not the place for that sort of thing at the moment.

He glanced over at us and nodded to some of the guys. "Well, congratulations, my little bitches. You win this round. Open those boxes in your hands. You will find the key in them. Go into the surf and wash off. Come back over here when you're done. Oh, and if any of you feel the stupid need to make a break for it, we are miles from any sort of civilization and you're all naked. So be smart and play along."

He turned and walked over to the pit where the guy was still feebly shoveling. I saw him squat down at the edge of the pit. I wanted to see what was going to happen to the guy there, but one of the muscled dudes was heading our way with a determined look on his face, so I quickly fumbled my box open.

The box was mostly full of cement, which explained the weight, and there on top was a key. I fumbled around with the back of my collar until I located a lock. I managed to get the damned thing off and flung it on the ground. The muscled guy was watching me with a smirk on his face. I would like to say I was defiant, but when you are naked and covered in sand, the best look you can hope for is pissy. I wandered toward the ocean, ignoring the other guys; they were doing the same. I just wanted to win and get the hell out of here.

When I had rinsed off as much of the sand as I could, I walked back to shore where the muscled morons were standing. One turned and walked back up to where we had come from. As we approached the hole, I noticed that there was now a marquee over the area. The hole also had the edges of a tarp around it and someone was laying some boards across the middle. I went to walk over, but a grunt from the genetic throwback in front of me told me this would be ill-advised.

He walked into a large tent that had been erected nearby (busy people, this bunch.) I followed. No sooner had I lifted the flap and entered the tent, then another bucket full of cold water hit me face on. I stood there naked, dripping and gasping in shock, while my gorilla guard laughed.

He finally stopped and pointed to a pile of rubber sitting on a table. "We got all that salt water off you. Now, get into that and head back to where you came from."

He walked out past me and I glared at his back. I muttered comments about the time it would take to shave an ape and teach it to talk, admittedly not loud enough for said ape to hear.

I wandered over and picked up the rubber item. It was a cat suit. It had attached hands and feet and a hood flopped against the front of it. I noticed a bottle of lube sitting beside the table, grabbed it, squeezed a liberal amount on the inside and then pulled the catsuit on. I felt the tight rubber grip my still-wet legs as I pulled the bottom half into place. I could feel the temperature inside the suit start to rise even when I only had it half on, and of course, as soon as I caught a whiff of that sweat and rubber smell, I got a rock hard-on.

I heard others enter and get the same bucket treatment. I didn't bother turning to watch. I managed to squeeze into the torso part of the suit and reached behind me and pulled the zipper up. I stretched the neck of the hood wide and pulled it over my face. There were mouth and nose holes, as well as pinhole eye holes. Once I had moved around a little and got the rubber to settle in place, I walked back outside and over to the hole.

The pit had been dug to an even depth and lined with a black tarp. At the bottom lay a guy dressed in a rubber cat suit like mine. He had black duct tape binding his ankles and knees together, and duct tape taped his arms to his side at the wrists and elbows. I assumed it was the guy who finished last. Unlike my suit, however, his mask was a gasmask with a clear visor from the nose up. His eyes were very wide and he looked scared as hell. My penis twitched in my rubbers. A hose ran from the mask up through a hole in the boards which had been placed over the pit, to the base of…a urinal.

It seemed that our lad was to be the toilet for a party. The dude wasn't kidding when he said there was penalties for failing.

Brett grinned as he watched the slaves line up and look down in the pit at the figure at the bottom, their unlucky teammate. He waited until the four slaves had all gathered before he spoke. "Well, as you see, your former teammate is going to be providing his service as a waste disposal unit." He waved at the muscled guards off to the side and one stepped up to each lad. "And now we will be leaving our friend here while we continue on our journey. But, if you will excuse me for one moment…" Brett walked onto the boards and unzipped his pants.

I was mesmerized by the guy at the bottom of the pit. He was squirming and bucking his hips. Every now and again, he would shake his head back and forth. When Brett had finished speaking and stepped onto the boards, he *really* began to struggle, trying to roll from side to side.

From the looks of things, though, he had been laid in an indent in the sand under the rubber and couldn't manage to roll up the side of it. I diverted my gaze to see Brett let loose a stream of piss into the urinal. The effect on the boy below was immediate -- a slight pause, and then bucking, moaning and gagging noises like you wouldn't believe.

I heard one of the guys next to me give a small laugh. I would bet money that it was my sworn enemy (hey, friends take a while to make; enemies are made in seconds.)

This poor guy was obviously not a piss fan. I had a feeling that by the end of the night he would be even less fond of it. Then again, better him than me. The gorilla behind me gave me a push and pointed over to an area where a heap of trucks and cars were parked. I started walking. The sand felt really weird under my rubber-covered feet. We were directed into the back of one of the trucks. As my eyes adjusted to the gloom, I saw that the back was empty, but there were large, black sacks lying on the floor near the walls.

The meathead behind me gave me another push toward one, and a sneaking suspicion of what lay ahead for me began to form. My suspicion was confirmed when he pulled open the neck of one and held it open and low for me to step into. I sighed.

Up close, I could see the sack was leather. It was already swelteringly hot in the back of the truck. It was worse because we were in rubbers. Sitting in a leather sack was not going to make my day noticeably better. Then again, if I hesitated too long, they might decide that two urinals would serve better than one, so I lifted my leg and stepped into the sack.

Ten minutes later, four hooded heads poked out of four leather sacks. At that point, we found out that there were hooks on the sides of the trucks. Because we were each lifted up and our bags hung from them, the weight of our bodies pulling down now trapped us in the bags. My guy gave me a grin and a slap on the cheek before he turned and walked out of the truck. I so wished I was holding that cement-filled box about now!

The truck trip was not very eventful. One of the dudes was trying to say something about us rushing the guards when we were let out. Now that should make for a interesting show; we all ignored him. I think each of us was thinking of ways to ensure we could win.

True to his word, that guy made an attempt to rush his guard when he was released. Even though we were all in identical rubber outfits and about the same height and build, it was easy to tell which one he was because he was still swaying from the whack around the head he had received for his efforts.

Brett stood smiling in front of a table piled up with four piles of metal, each next to a bucket. We all wandered over. Brett flashed us a grin and I had a sudden image, similar to oh, what the last image most mice would see must be like. He then made a wide, waving gesture over the four piles of metal. "Welcome, welcome. I hope you had an enjoyable trip."

I snorted as I rubbed the side of my leg. The truck had taken a corner a little fast and my bag had swung away from the wall and then slammed back against it again. I knew I would have a large bruise on that leg. Brett either didn't hear me, or ignored me, but my assigned Neanderthal gave me a warning poke in the back. Ten minutes with a baseball bat -- if only I could've had one wish granted in my life, that would have been it.

I looked around to see what kind of place we were in. The arrangement of the tables and couches suggested a restaurant; the bar at the end of the room suggested this was a club. Brett folded his hands behind his back and continued talking. "You all need to put together the items in front of you here. The tools you need are in the buckets. Begin!"

With that, he wandered over to the side. We all paused for half a second, then raced toward the table. Since my leg was still aching from the whack it received, I was a little slower. However, the valiant idiot behind me who had been whacked in the head was slower still. I managed to get to a spot and looked in the bucket. It was full of clear, amber liquid. There were a number of screwdrivers at the bottom. Oh well, at least the tools were simple.

I quickly organized the pile in front of me. The ends that had to go together were marked with color-coded dots. I pushed all the same-colored dots together.

In front of me was the following -- two halves of what looked like wrist or ankle restraints. Each half was shaped like a lower-case "W" so that when both halves were placed together you had a figure 8-style cuff. One half of that had to attach to a long, straight piece of metal. About halfway down that, a semi-circle of metal had to be attached on the opposite side as the cuff half. The end of the long piece of metal then had to have two chains screwed into it. At the end of each chain was another, smaller semi-circle of metal. To the side were colored screws and bolts in little containers. This would be easy.

I realized how tricky it was going to be when I plunged my hand into the bucket to grab a screwdriver. The liquid was thick and slippery. OIL! Oh, *SHIT!*

I pulled out all the screwdrivers and placed them on the bench beside the bucket of oil and tried to shake my hands to get the excess off them. This was going to be tricky. The screws were rather small, and picking them up with rubber-covered, oily hands was not going to be an easy task. The bolts were a little easier, but harder to tighten because your fingers kept slipping on the grips. The screwdrivers were also very smooth, so getting everything to screw in properly was going to be a challenge as well. Once I got going I found it was even harder than I thought. I kept dropping screws and bolts, and they rolled off the edge. Getting the screws to sit in place was a nightmare, and so was having to peer through the pinpricks to look at the heads of the screws to see which screwdriver to use. To top it off, some sick bastard had made it so that the color of the handle of the screwdriver did not match the color of the screw, and of course when you're trying to put a red screw into a hole with a red dot next to it, you automatically reach for a red screwdriver.

The guy next to me bumped me when I had just positioned the screw over the semi-circle of metal under the straight bar. I glared at him; was it the same fuckhead who had thrown dirt in my hole? I didn't know, but I picked up another screw and continued watching him out of the corner of my eye. At one stage he picked up one of the chains to screw in place and it slipped through his hands onto the floor. He bent over to pick it up and I quickly reached over and grabbed the screwdriver he would need and tossed it back in the bucket of oil. He would soon learn, or if it was not him -- *everyone* would soon learn that trying to sabotage me would only come back to bite you in the ass.

I managed finally to tighten the last bolt with my slippery fingers, the one holding the chains to the end of the long piece of metal. I stepped back and put up my hands to show I was finished. I looked around; the dude beside me had finished before me again, despite me trying to slow him down. The two dudes left were both on their last bolt; this was going to be close. The one on the right went to give his bolt a hard twist and his fingers slipped off. He fumbled with the whole thing for a few seconds, which gave the other dude enough time to complete his last turn of the screw and step back.

The guy on the right seemed to slump down and go limp. Brett stepped forward and placed a hand on his shoulder as if to comfort him, but his grin was pure evil. His tone was mocking as he spoke. "Ooooh, so close, yet so far. Oh well, don't worry. For putting in such a good effort, we have a special prize for you." Nothing about his smile or tone suggested this was an improvement in any way, and this was confirmed when one of the other dudes stepped forward, carrying another metal object.

This one was like the ones we had just put together and which I suspected we would soon be wearing. It had a longer, straight piece of metal and there weren't the two halves of the restraints, which I figured is where out hands would probably be placed. At one end of the long piece was a smaller semi-circle that I suspected was half of a collar. The large semi-circle in the middle was where I suspected another half would be placed to form a belt.

However, instead of two small semi-circles at the ends of the chains attached to the end of the long piece of metal, there was a figure 8-style restraint at the end of each chain. One circle was really large, wider than the collar but not as wide as the belt; the other was smaller. Instead of each circle being right next to each other, there was a flat space, so it looked more like O-o.

Two muscled guards grabbed the dude, and he immediately started to struggle, kick and scream. One seemed to be fiddling with parts of the metal restraint while the other was holding the guy still as best he could. Brett walked forward, and as the guy opened his mouth to yell again, Brett stuffed a gag in his mouth and buckled it closed. The muffled complaint continued, but he had no chance against the two men holding him.

First, they positioned the whole thing at his back. The wide semi-circle did indeed form part of a belt, and they screwed the other half in place. The dude holding him wrapped one arm around the top of his head as the dude screwed the second half of his collar in place. He then reached down and grabbed the restraints on the end of the chains. He unscrewed the two halves and then placed half the wide 'O' around the guy's thigh, screwing the two halves together loosely, and then repeated the process with the other leg. He then grabbed one of the dude's legs that was kicking around and bent it at the knee all the way back until he got the ankle up to the small 'o' and pulled the loosely-joined halves together to place the ankle between it. Then he tightened it and did the same with the other ankle.

The dude holding him had wrapped his arms around the dude's waist while the dude was trying to punch at both him and the other dude tightening the metal onto him. They both ignored him. When the two halves of both ankle/thigh restraints were in place, the guy holding him lowered him down and then walked over to a bench nearby. The guy tried to get up, but couldn't, because his ankles were attached to his thighs. He pushed himself up so he was kneeling, and tried to reach behind himself to feel for the screws around the ankles and thighs. The collar prevented him from turning his head too much. The dude near him gave him a shove and forced him on all fours again.

The other dude returned with an armful of leather gear. First he grabbed the dude's hands and forced them into a pair of puppy mitts. His hands were now useless for manipulating screws. He then strapped kneepads onto the dude's knees, ignoring the guy trying to hit him with his padded hands. Finally, he moved behind the guy and fiddled with the bottom of the suit. My own hand wandered to the bottom of my suit and I found that there was a zipper down there. The guy then held up a tail butt plug, and with no lube or anything, crammed it into the guy's butt. The howl of pain the guy let out was very impressive. I had no idea anyone could make so much noise around a gag.

Brett stepped forward. "Well, it looks like we have the mascot for tonight's party. He will no doubt be very popular amongst all the guys when they arrive, particularly if he continues to behave like this. No doubt they will take him with them when they head to the beach party. They may even put him in the pit to keep his friend company."

The guy on the floor kept pushing himself up into a kneeling position and kept getting pushed down. Finally, one of the guys placed a boot on his back and he couldn't do it anymore. Brett watched this with a smile, then started talking again. "And now, because you all worked so hard to get these built, it seems only fair that you get to try them first."

While we had been watching the show, our guards grabbed the metal restraints off the table. I would like to say that I went down fighting, that I had to be forced into each segment; however, in the back of my mind, a little voice was saying, 'There is always room for one more dog or one more toilet,' and so I just stood there as my guard tightened the belt around my waist. As much as I disliked the guy, I was not immune to the fact that a large, well-muscled dude was basically hugging me, his head resting on my shoulder so he could see what he was doing. He must have noticed the bulge in the front of my rubber because he pulled me back against him while pretending to tighten the belt. From what I could feel rubbing against my ass, it seemed that somewhere out there, a horse had been robbed of its penis.

He didn't say anything, but when he pulled my hands behind me to place them in the restraints at the end of the bar, and he bent one arm up to put it in place, he placed the other on his groin.

He was wearing tight 501s and I ran my hand over the bulge beneath them. In my defense, I had just witnessed two very twisted, yet fucking hot, scenes of guys being tormented. I was in rubber and was surrounded by hot, muscled, and above all, *dumb* guys, my favorite combo.

He took a while getting my first wrist in place, and then reluctantly grabbed my other hand and bent it up into place. I felt the metal tighten and trap my wrists in an unyielding grip. Then he placed his hands on my shoulders and pushed down, indicating I should kneel. I did so and he placed one hand on my chest and pushed forward from the back, forcing me to lie down, a little tricky to do by yourself with your hands behind you. I saw one of the other dudes push a dude forward and was glad that I had resisted the temptation to be difficult. My ankles were grabbed, bent up and attached to the restraints at the end of the chains. Ta da! Instant hogtie.

I wiggled a little. It was not comfortable lying on the floor, but the restraints were not so tight that they bit into our skin. I heard wheels, and a trolley appeared near my head. I was lifted up and placed on it, and the other two dudes were put next to me. We were wheeled out and put back up into the back of the truck. The trolley wheels must have been lockable because we barely moved as we drove off to our next challenge.

When had been unloaded, wheeled inside, and placed on the floor, I had no idea where we were. Our hands were released, and I lay there waiting for my ankles to be undone.

Instead, I heard Brett's voice say, "Well, then, last challenge. Double elimination! Ready, set, go!"

I looked up. He was walking to the other end of the room where there was a small pillar. I frantically twisted and scrabbled at the bolts holding my ankle restraints together and heard the other two doing the same.

Luckily, while I had been rubbing my guard's crotch, I had wiped a lot of the oil off my rubber-covered hands, so I was able to get the bolts undone quickly. I stood up and quickly started to work on the bolts in the belt. The guy must have known what was next because the bolts were not all that tight. I take it back -- he was great, he was my best buddy, he could have free head jobs for the rest of his life, I didn't care. I just wanted this belt off fast.

On the floor, one dude was still playing with his first ankle restraint while the other had chosen to get the belt off first and was now sitting up and unscrewing his restraints.

The whole thing fell off me with a clunk and I was running. I heard footsteps behind me. The color of the oil was the same as the carpeting, so I didn't need to worry about any oil on my rubber-covered feet. I was half-running, half-jogging, since my thigh was still sore from the bruising I had gotten, but I had a good lead.

Brett watched. One of the boys got his ankle restraints off fast and then stood up and undid his belt, the guy beside him choosing to do his belt first. They were both getting them off fast, which meant they must have gone easy and submitted to the guards. Because obedience was rewarded, Brett had told the guards that any lads who struggled were to be bolted really tight, and those that did not were only to be loosely bolted in.

It was impossible to tell them all apart, of course, since they all were dressed head to toe in rubber. Boi #1, as Brett had nicknamed the first to stand, had finally freed himself of his belt and was off. He seemed to be limping, though; maybe he had a cramp from the position he had been in. Boi #2 had freed his ankles, rolled and launched himself in one smooth action, obviously saving his ankles for last to get a good starting position.

The last boy had barely managed to get one ankle free; he must have annoyed the guard. Boi #2 ran in smooth, long steps, and in no time he was level with Boi #1. Then his foot kicked out, and Boy #1 was suddenly on the ground, rolling head over heels.

Brett smiled -- a ruthless lad who would win at any cost; this boy was perfect.

It was me, however, that was in the lead. I was nearly there! I was going to wi...... *AAAAAWWGHHH!!*

My whole world was spinning around. I finally realized I was lying still on the ground. I managed to push myself up and stagger the last of the distance. I didn't care about finishing anymore; all I cared about was getting my hands around the neck of the guy who had tripped me, and then squeeze until he stopped struggling.

I launched myself at the guy yelling, and was grabbed from behind and held immobile against what felt like a wall -- a wall wearing a bad shirt, so I am guessing it was one of the guards. I was yelling and swearing at the fucker who had tripped me; he was standing there smirking.

Brett stepped forward and crammed a gag into my mouth mid-yell. He tightened it behind my head. This made me calm down a little and I relaxed in the grip of my guard. He loosened his grip, but still held me firmly.

Brett grabbed another gag and walked over to the right. I turned my head and saw that the guy had been carried to the end, still in his restraints, and was being released now. He was gagged, and Brett stepped back and put his arm around the shoulders of the winner, who was still staring right at me, smirking. I was having that baseball bat wish again.

"Well, now, that was an interesting finish. To the losers, good effort, but not good enough. Now, if I can direct your attention to the pictures on that wall over there."

I was turned to face the wall by my guard. Over on the side were two paintings. They were not landscapes or anything. They stretched from floor to ceiling, whirls of color and spirals, the classic 'my two year old could paint this' style. Amazing that there are so many talented two-year-olds running around considering the apparent depth of the gene pool they had been spawned from.

My wandering mind was brought back to the present when Brett walked over and pressed a section of wall near each painting. They suddenly disappeared and I was looking at two alcoves, each with a number of leather straps running up the back wall. As I was moved closer, I saw that the paintings hadn't disappeared but that there was now glass where the paintings had been.

Brett explained that it was a style of two-way glass. The glass was actually two panes with a layer of liquid crystal between them; when a current ran through the crystal, the pattern we had seen appeared on one side. Then I remembered what the pattern reminded me of -- it was like when you press on a calculator screen and see those whirls of color. Brett pressed another part and the glass swung forward slightly. I knew what was coming next.

I watched Brett swing the glass back into place and I bit down hard on my gag to alleviate my frustration; I had been so close. I tried to move a little to get comfortable. The leather straps held me against the wall at my ankles, just above my knees, my waist, across my chest, my neck, and finally one over my fore-head. My arms were held in place in front of me with a pair of cuffs attached to the belt around my waist; fist mitts had been put over my hands so I couldn't use them to undo the straps. The back wall was heavily padded, and the straps had padding on the side, touching the body so I was comfortable standing there. But I was so pissed off. I watched through the glass as Brett chatted to the guy as he stripped off his rubber suit. It was the same fucker who had thrown dirt in my hole. He was smiling and chatting to Brett, who was standing, nodding with his arms crossed. Brett grinned, said something, and the dude's expression changed to that of confusion.

Suddenly, two guards grabbed him. Hello, hello, what was this all about, then?

Brett smiled again. "That's right. You're the fittest, smart-est, and most capable slave out of the five I selected -- from masters who have very high standards. You will be the perfect present for my friend on his birthday."

The guy was struggling against the two guards. He was trying to talk around the gag they had stuffed in his mouth. Brett waved a hand. "Oh, it's okay. Don't thank me. My friend is look-ing for a new 24/7 slave. You will do nicely, I'm sure. No doubt, you will need some training to get used to your new, and may I say, *permanent* role, but you have all the basics, which is impor-tant. Now, let's get you wrapped up."

The boy struggled furiously as he was stuffed into a leather sleep sack, which was laced up tightly, causing the struggling to grow less and less intense. Brett knelt beside the head sticking out at the end -- the boy's eyes were nearly perfectly round, the whites showing all the way around.

Brett smiled at the lad again. "Congratulations, again, on winning." He then pulled a leather bag hood over the boy's face. He stood back and let two guards wrap a red ribbon around the middle of the leather sleep sack and place a bow where the two ends met. Brett leaned down and slipped the card to his friend under the ribbon. He stood, and two guards lifted a couch up, placing it over the top of the struggling figure.

I stood watching. Brett strolled over to the pictures as the guards had been lowering the couch into place, and pressed something near the picture. The glass had gone a little hazy, but I could still see through it. Brett must have sent the current through the liquid crystal.

Some time passed and some people started to arrive. They passed in front of the 'paintings,' gazing at them, sometimes talking in front of me. It was weird knowing I could see them. It seemed that this was a formal party, but more and more guests left until there was a group of about forty guys standing around. When the last couple had left, everyone scattered.

There had been waiters carrying trays around all night. They reappeared but now they wore only "G"-strings and leather caps. Guests reappeared, but now in leather gear. My cock sprung awake again at the sight of all this. Brett lifted the couch off the leather sleep-sacked guy and everyone was slapping one dude on the back and laughing.

Brett wandered over to the 'paintings' and the glass went completely clear. Everyone wandered over and crowded around, leering obviously at me and the dude next to me. After a while, everyone started to trickle out, no doubt heading to the club where the mascot waited, then to the beach to empty their bladders, which would by then be very full.

And then, suddenly there was Richard!!! YAAAAAAAAAAAAY.

He walked up to Brett and looked very annoyed. After some arm waving and talking, they both turned toward me.

An alarm beeped near me. I groaned and reached over until I found the source of the noise and switched it off. My brain then reminded me I didn't have an alarm.

I sat upright and looked around. I was in a jeep, the driver's side seat was down. I was covered in a blanket. Well, this wasn't too bad. Outside it was dark; there were no lights around, but there was a small, glowing, battery-operated lamp near me filling the car with a soft glow.

I reached up and flicked on the roof light. As I moved, I felt constriction around my groin -- oh no, not again. Sure enough, when I flung aside the blanket, I was once again encased in metal.

I sighed. This was no longer laughable, at least not when viewed objectively, anyway. I noticed two envelopes on the seat next to me. One had my name written on it in elegant script. I guessed it was from Richard and opened it. It was a apology note. He felt ashamed that I had been removed from his care and nearly come to harm. He apologized for about two paragraphs for the way I had to be transported home. He had not been able to organize the documentation and felt that he could not keep me any longer after what had happened.

Then, at the bottom, as an apology, he told me the jeep was mine. Well, talk about actions speaking louder then words!!! This however, didn't explain why I was in this belt. The next letter, however, did.

Slave,

Uncle Richard told me about you. You sound like fun. I want another shot at you. Be at this address Thursday, two weeks from now.

Brett

Oh, Lordy, here we go again.

ABOUT THE AUTHOR

Shadow was born and bred and lives as a not-so-innocent country boy in the wilds of Australia. At 24, with much experience in the areas of BDSM, his writing is well known in his home country, mostly on the Internet.

Shadow is planning on visiting the US and Canada in 2007.

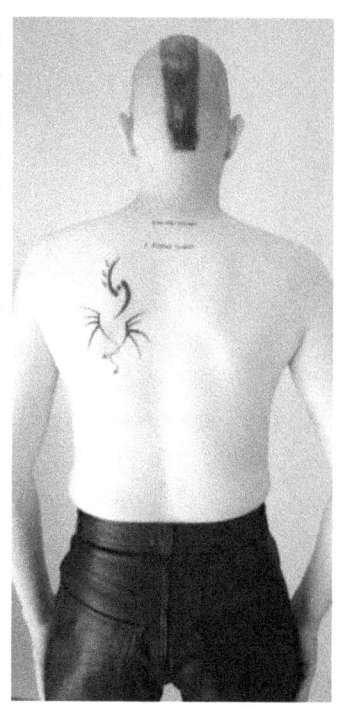

www.ingramcontent.com/pod-product-compliance
Lightning Source LLC
Chambersburg PA
CBHW071226260626
47162CB00004B/1435